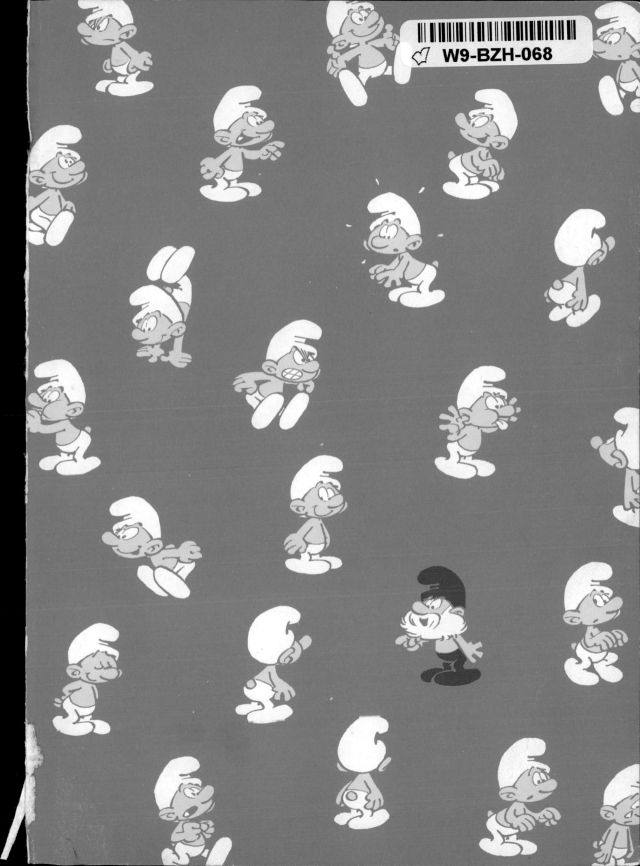

THE SMURFS AND THE MAGIC FLUTE

Peyo

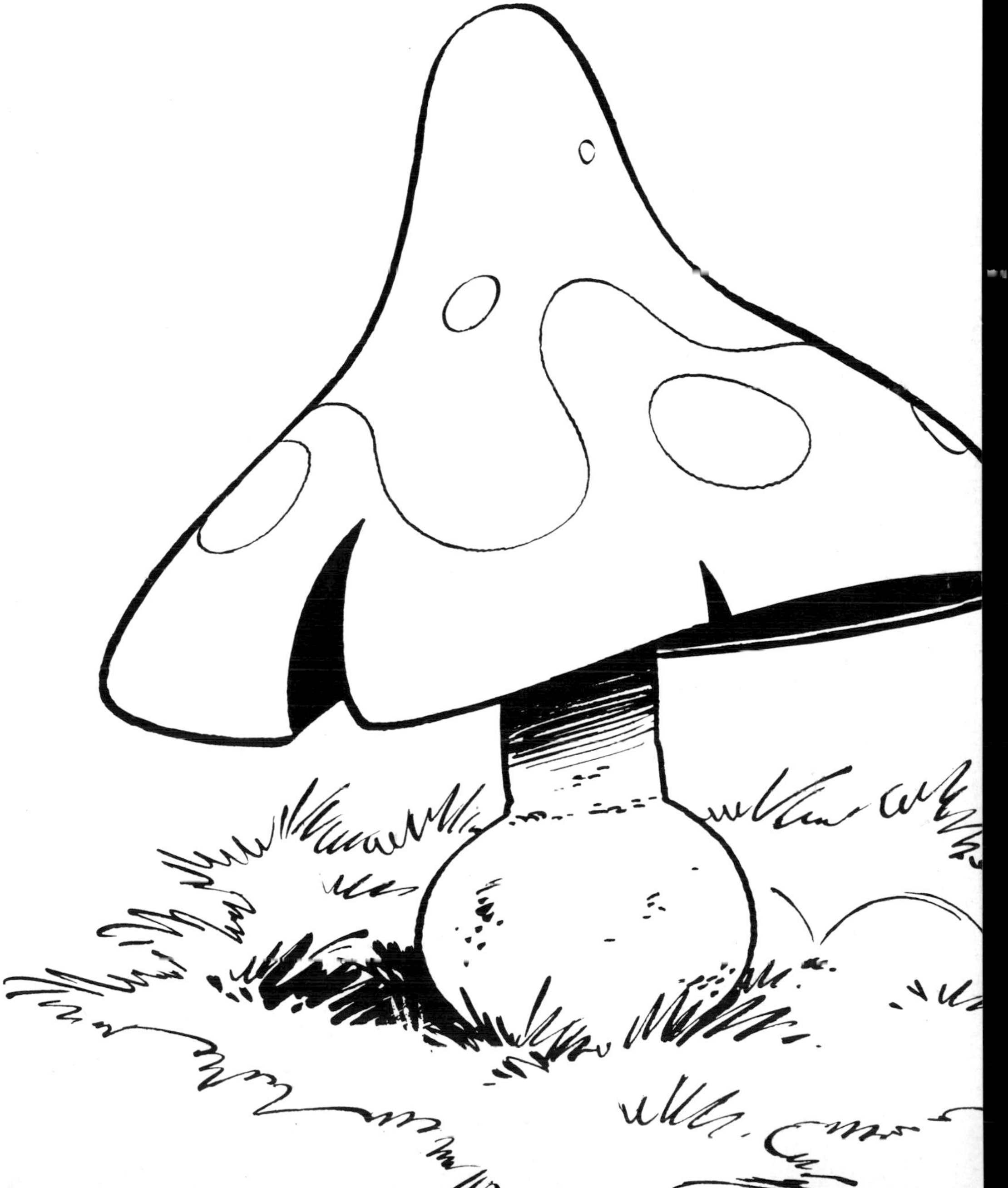

THE S
MA(

A

MURFS AND THE GIC FLUTE

What are they smurfing here?
They sure look smurfy!
Peyo 57

SMURFS GRAPHIC NOVEL BY Peyo

PAPERCUTZ™
NEW YORK

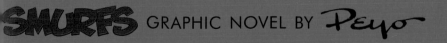

SMURFS GRAPHIC NOVELS
AVAILABLE FROM PAPERCUTZ™

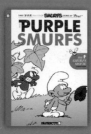

GRAPHIC NOVEL NO. 1:
THE PURPLE SMURFS

GRAPHIC NOVEL NO. 2:
THE SMURFS AND THE MAGIC FLUTE

COMING SOON:

GRAPHIC NOVEL NO. 3:
THE SMURF KING

The Smurfs graphic novels are available in paperback for $5.99 each and in hardcover for $10.99 each. Please add $4.00 for postage and handling for the first book, add $1.00 for each additional book.

Please make check payable to:
NBM Publishing

Send to:
PAPERCUTZ, 40 Exchange Place, Suite 1308
New York, NY 10005 [1-800-886-1223]

WWW.PAPERCUTZ.COM

THE SMURFS AND THE MAGIC FLUTE

Smurf™ © Peyo - 2010 - Licensed through Lafig Belgium

English translation Copyright © 2010 by Papercutz.
All rights reserved.

"The Smurfs and the Magic Flute"
BY YVAN DELPORTE AND PEYO

Joe Johnson, SMURFLATIONS
Adam Grano, SMURFIC DESIGN
Janice Chiang, LETTERING SMURFETTE
Michael Petranek, ASSISTANT SMURF
Matt. Murray, SMURF CONSULTANT
Jim Salicrup, SMURF-IN-CHIEF

PAPERBACK EDITION ISBN: 978-1-59707-208-3
HARDCOVER EDITION ISBN: 978-1-59707-209-6

PRINTED IN CHINA JUNE 2010 BY WKT CO. LTD.
3/F PHASE I LEADER INDUSTRIAL CENTRE
188 TEXACO ROAD, TSEUN WAN, N.T., HONG KONG

DISTRIBUTED BY MACMILLAN
FIRST PRINTING

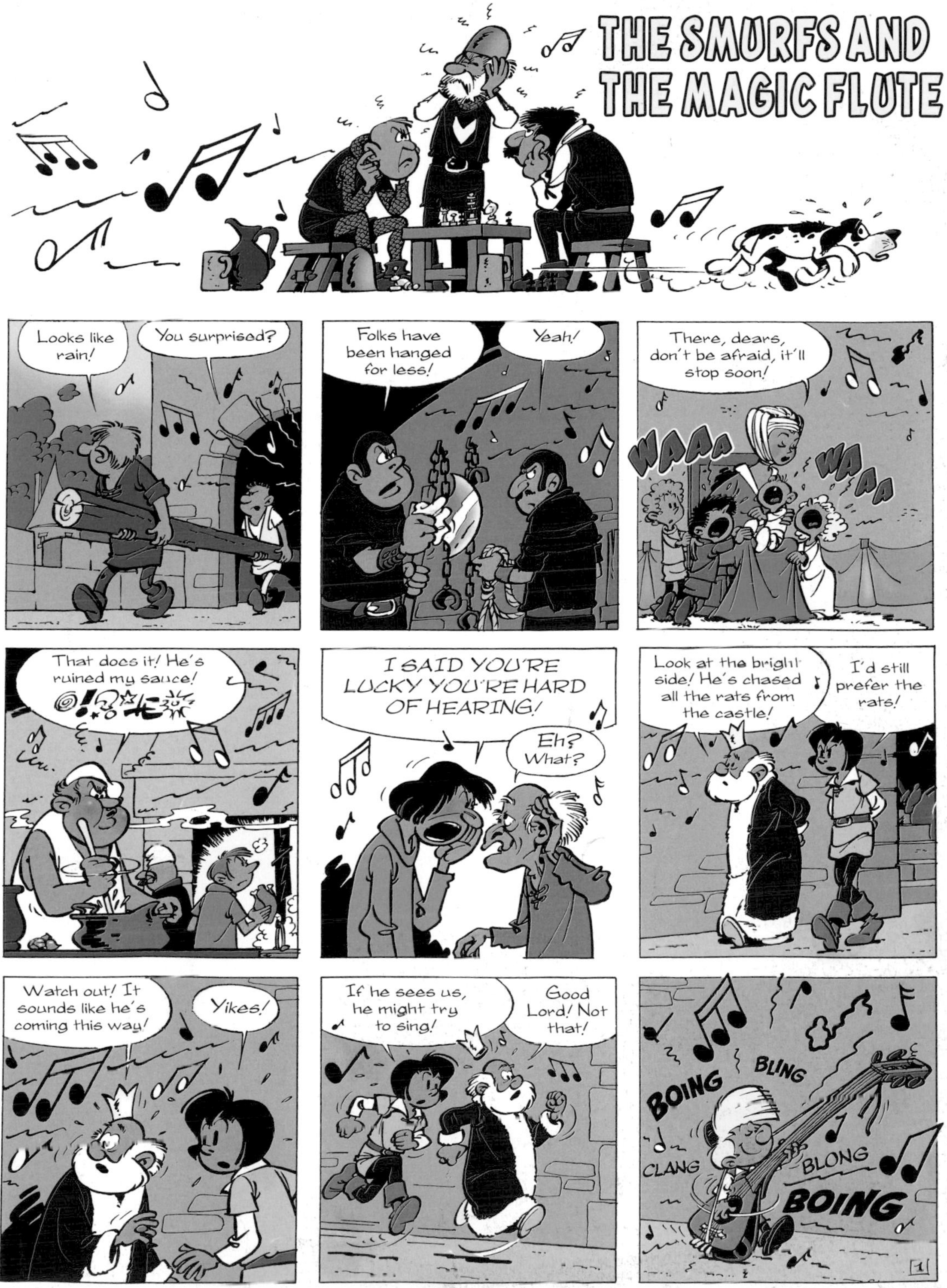
THE SMURFS AND THE MAGIC FLUTE
Looks like rain!
You surprised?
Folks have been hanged for less!
Yeah!
There, dears, don't be afraid, it'll stop soon!
WAAA
WAAA
That does it! He's ruined my sauce!
I SAID YOU'RE LUCKY YOU'RE HARD OF HEARING!
Eh? What?
Look at the bright side! He's chased all the rats from the castle!
I'd still prefer the rats!
Watch out! It sounds like he's coming this way!
Yikes!
If he sees us, he might try to sing!
Good Lord! Not that!
BOING
BLING
CLANG
BLONG
BOING
1

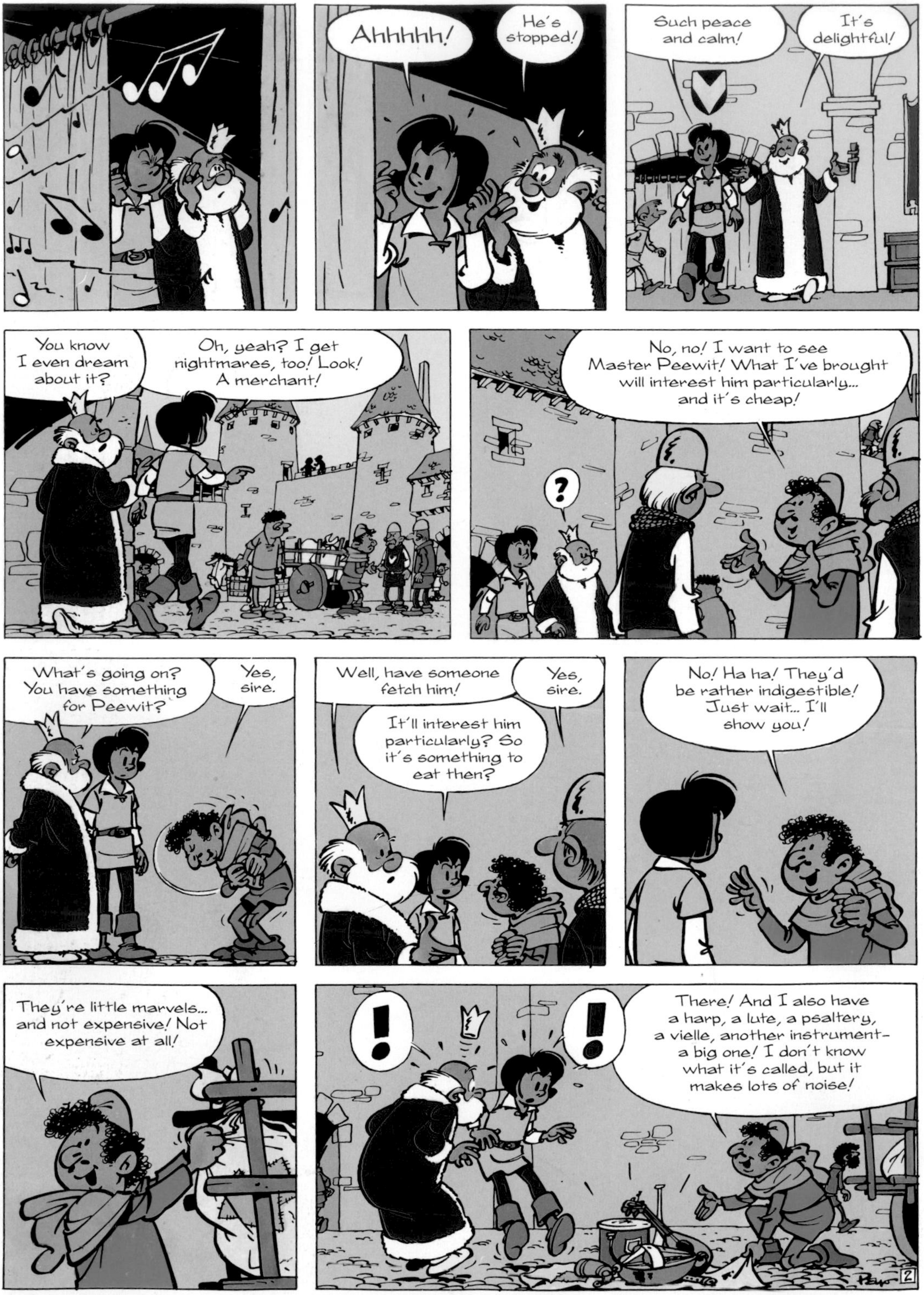
Ahhhhh!
He's stopped!
Such peace and calm!
It's delightful!
You know I even dream about it?
Oh, yeah? I get nightmares, too! Look! A merchant!
?
No, no! I want to see Master Peewit! What I've brought will interest him particularly... and it's cheap!
What's going on? You have something for Peewit?
Yes, sire.
Well, have someone fetch him!
Yes, sire.
It'll interest him particularly? So it's something to eat then?
No! Ha ha! They'd be rather indigestible! Just wait... I'll show you!
They're little marvels... and not expensive! Not expensive at all!
!
!
There! And I also have a harp, a lute, a psaltery, a vielle, another instrument– a big one! I don't know what it's called, but it makes lots of noise!
2

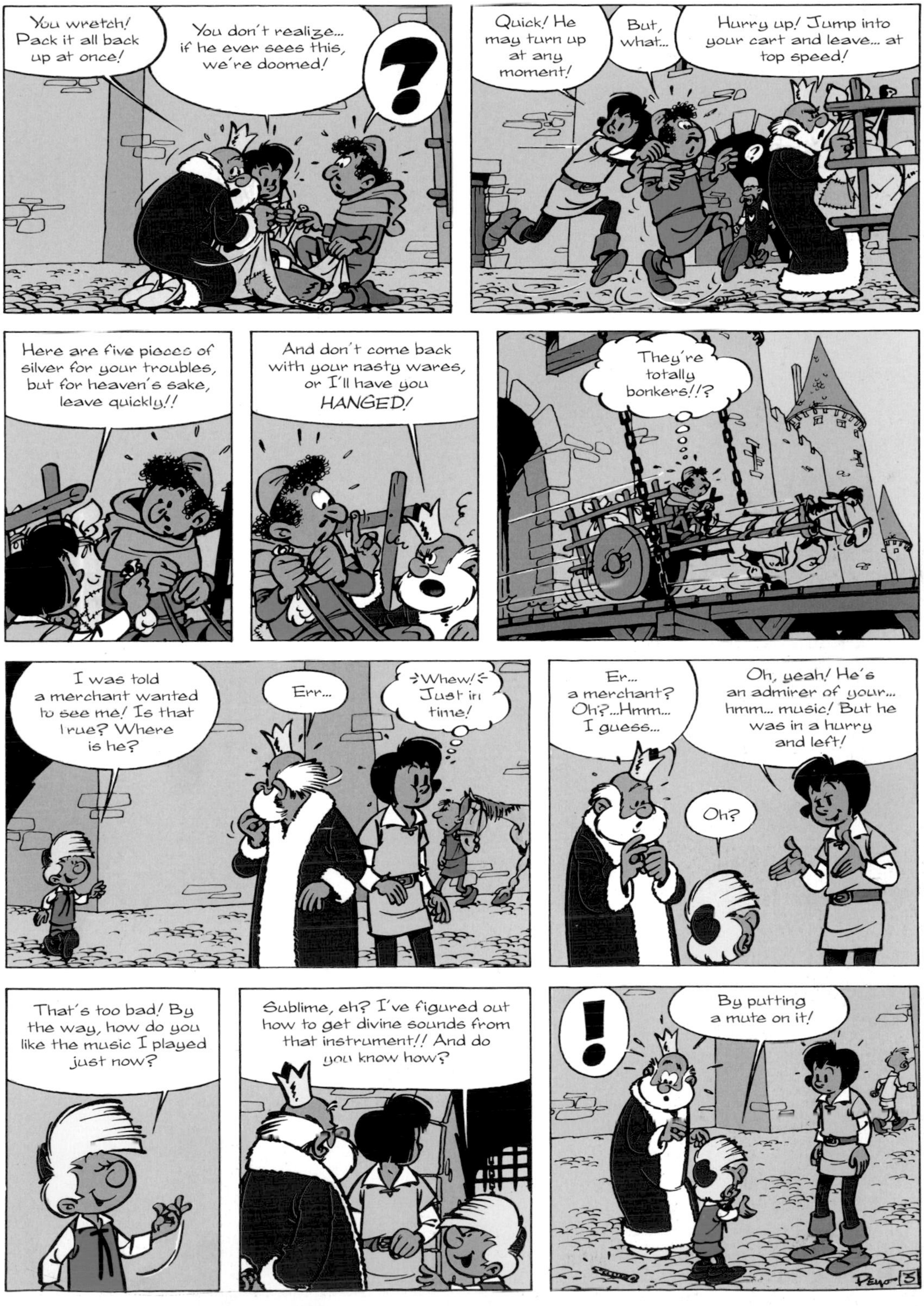
You wretch! Pack it all back up at once!
You don't realize... if he ever sees this, we're doomed!
?
Quick! He may turn up at any moment!
But, what...
Hurry up! Jump into your cart and leave... at top speed!
Here are five pieces of silver for your troubles, but for heaven's sake, leave quickly!!
And don't come back with your nasty wares, or I'll have you HANGED!
They're totally bonkers!!?
I was told a merchant wanted to see me! Is that true? Where is he?
Err...
Whew! Just in time!
Er... a merchant? Oh?...Hmm... I guess...
Oh, yeah! He's an admirer of your... hmm... music! But he was in a hurry and left!
Oh?
That's too bad! By the way, how do you like the music I played just now?
Sublime, eh? I've figured out how to get divine sounds from that instrument!! And do you know how?
!
By putting a mute on it!
3

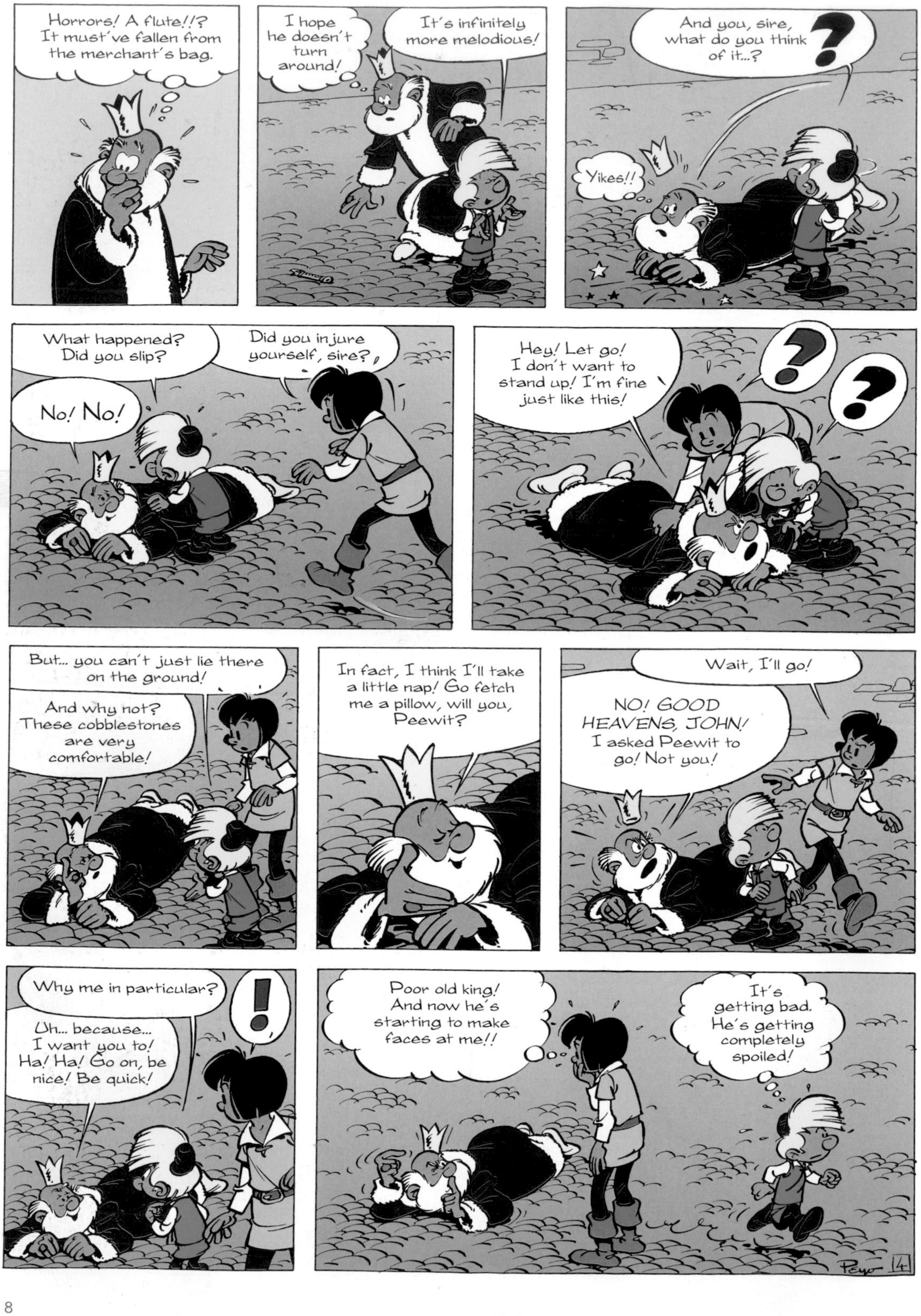

Horrors! A flute!!? It must've fallen from the merchant's bag.
I hope he doesn't turn around!
It's infinitely more melodious!
And you, sire, what do you think of it...?
Yikes!!
What happened? Did you slip?
Did you injure yourself, sire?
No! No!
Hey! Let go! I don't want to stand up! I'm fine just like this!
But... you can't just lie there on the ground!
And why not? These cobblestones are very comfortable!
In fact, I think I'll take a little nap! Go fetch me a pillow, will you, Peewit?
Wait, I'll go!
NO! GOOD HEAVENS, JOHN! I asked Peewit to go! Not you!
Why me in particular?
Uh... because... I want you to! Ha! Ha! Go on, be nice! Be quick!
Poor old king! And now he's starting to make faces at me!!
It's getting bad. He's getting completely spoiled!
Peyo
14

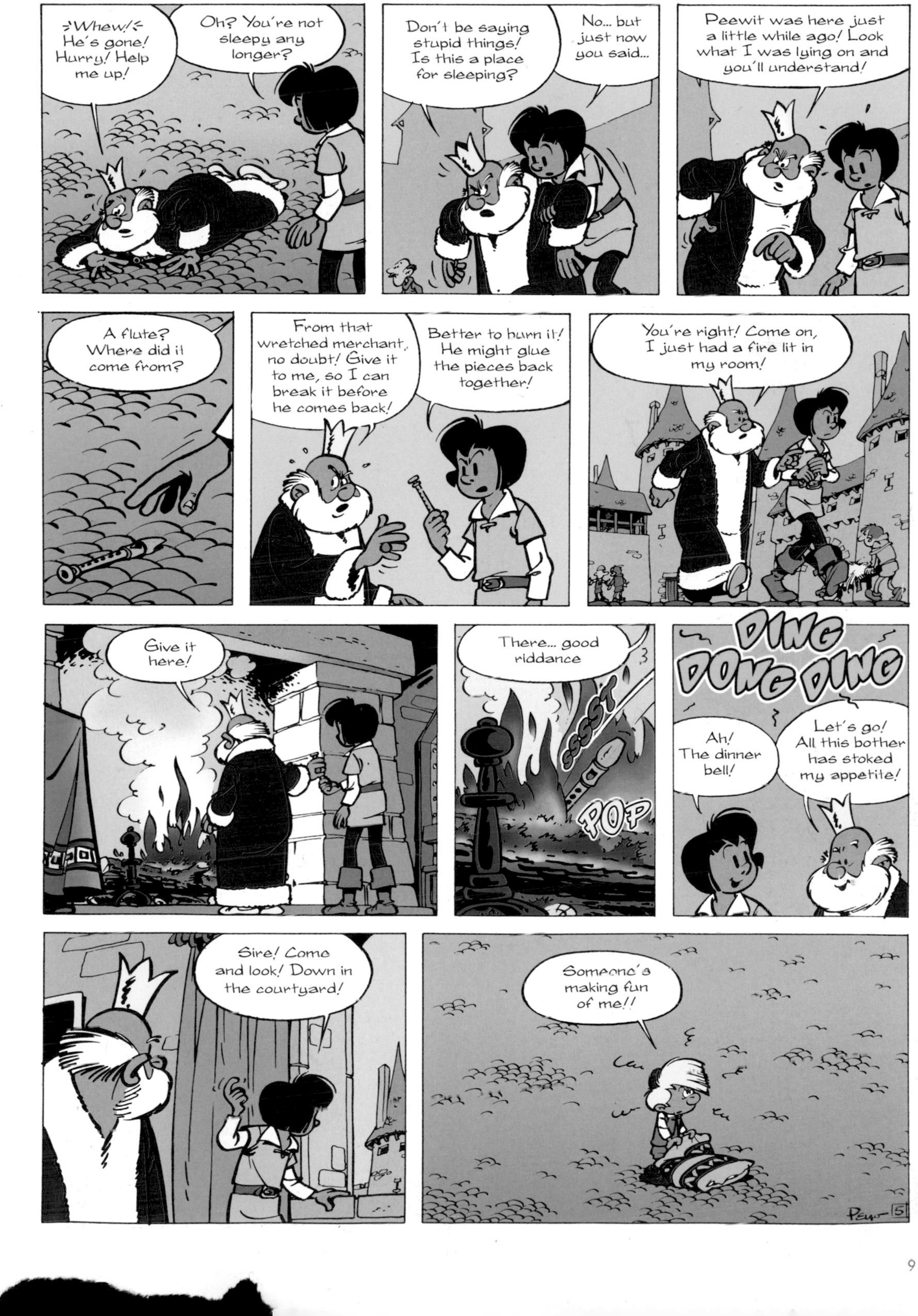
Whew! He's gone! Hurry! Help me up!
Oh? You're not sleepy any longer?
Don't be saying stupid things! Is this a place for sleeping?
No... but just now you said...
Peewit was here just a little while ago! Look what I was lying on and you'll understand!
A flute? Where did it come from?
From that wretched merchant, no doubt! Give it to me, so I can break it before he comes back!
Better to burn it! He might glue the pieces back together!
You're right! Come on, I just had a fire lit in my room!
Give it here!
There... good riddance
SSSST
POP
DING DONG DING
Ah! The dinner bell!
Let's go! All this bother has stoked my appetite!
Sire! Come and look! Down in the courtyard!
Someone's making fun of me!!

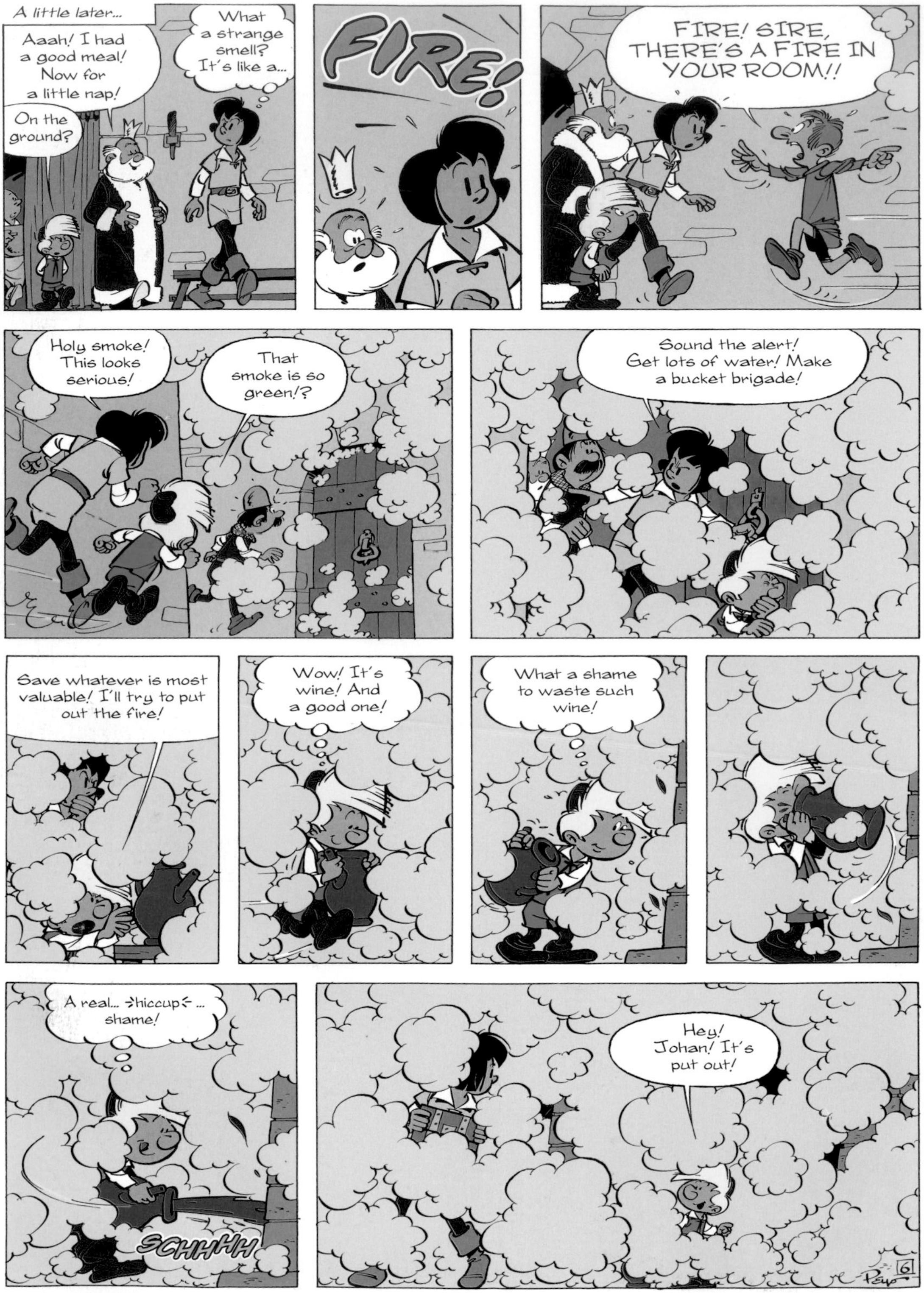
A little later...
Aaah! I had a good meal! Now for a little nap!
What a strange smell? It's like a...
On the ground?
FIRE!
FIRE! SIRE, THERE'S A FIRE IN YOUR ROOM!!
Holy smoke! This looks serious!
That smoke is so green!?
Sound the alert! Get lots of water! Make a bucket brigade!
Save whatever is most valuable! I'll try to put out the fire!
Wow! It's wine! And a good one!
What a shame to waste such wine!
A real... *hiccup* ... shame!
SCHHHH
Hey! Johan! It's put out!

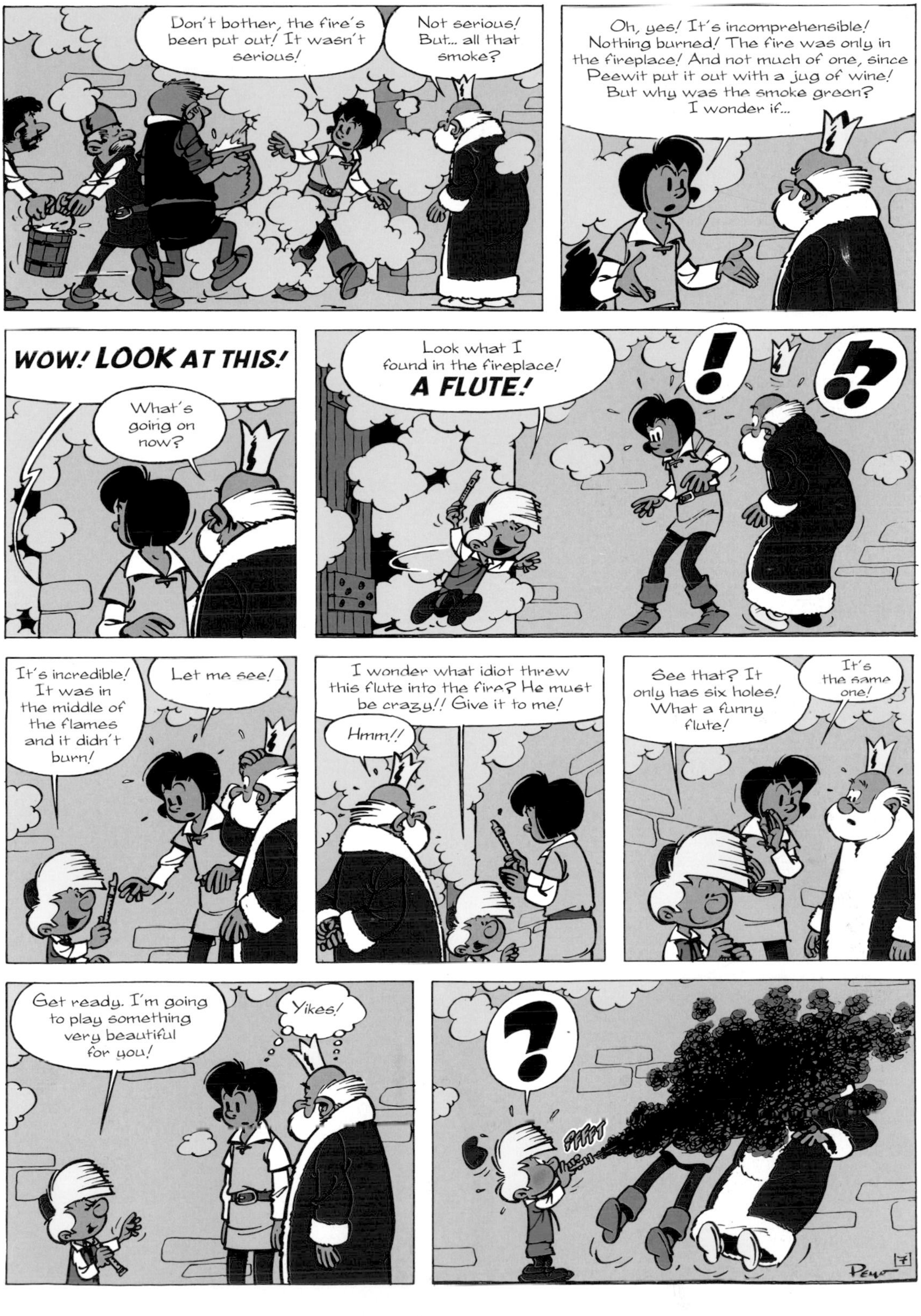
Don't bother, the fire's been put out! It wasn't serious!
Not serious! But... all that smoke?
Oh, yes! It's incomprehensible! Nothing burned! The fire was only in the fireplace! And not much of one, since Peewit put it out with a jug of wine! But why was the smoke green? I wonder if...
WOW! LOOK AT THIS!
What's going on now?
Look what I found in the fireplace! A FLUTE!
It's incredible! It was in the middle of the flames and it didn't burn!
Let me see!
I wonder what idiot threw this flute into the fire? He must be crazy!! Give it to me!
Hmm!!
See that? It only has six holes! What a funny flute!
It's the same one!
Get ready. I'm going to play something very beautiful for you!
Yikes!
PFFFT

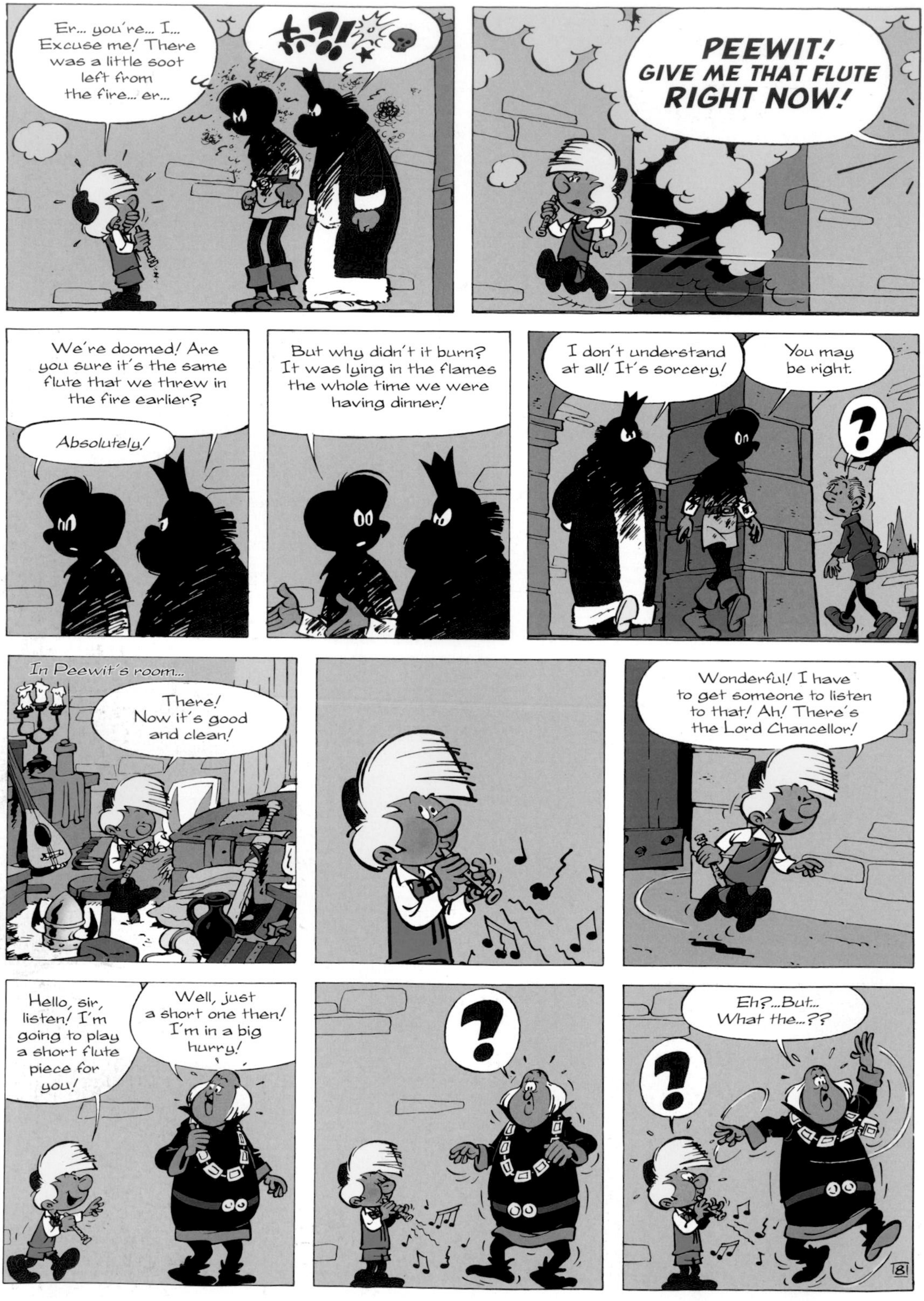
Er... you're... I... Excuse me! There was a little soot left from the fire... er...
PEEWIT! GIVE ME THAT FLUTE RIGHT NOW!
We're doomed! Are you sure it's the same flute that we threw in the fire earlier?
Absolutely!
But why didn't it burn? It was lying in the flames the whole time we were having dinner!
I don't understand at all! It's sorcery!
You may be right.
In Peewit's room...
There! Now it's good and clean!
Wonderful! I have to get someone to listen to that! Ah! There's the Lord Chancellor!
Hello, sir, listen! I'm going to play a short flute piece for you!
Well, just a short one then! I'm in a big hurry!
Eh?...But... What the...??
8

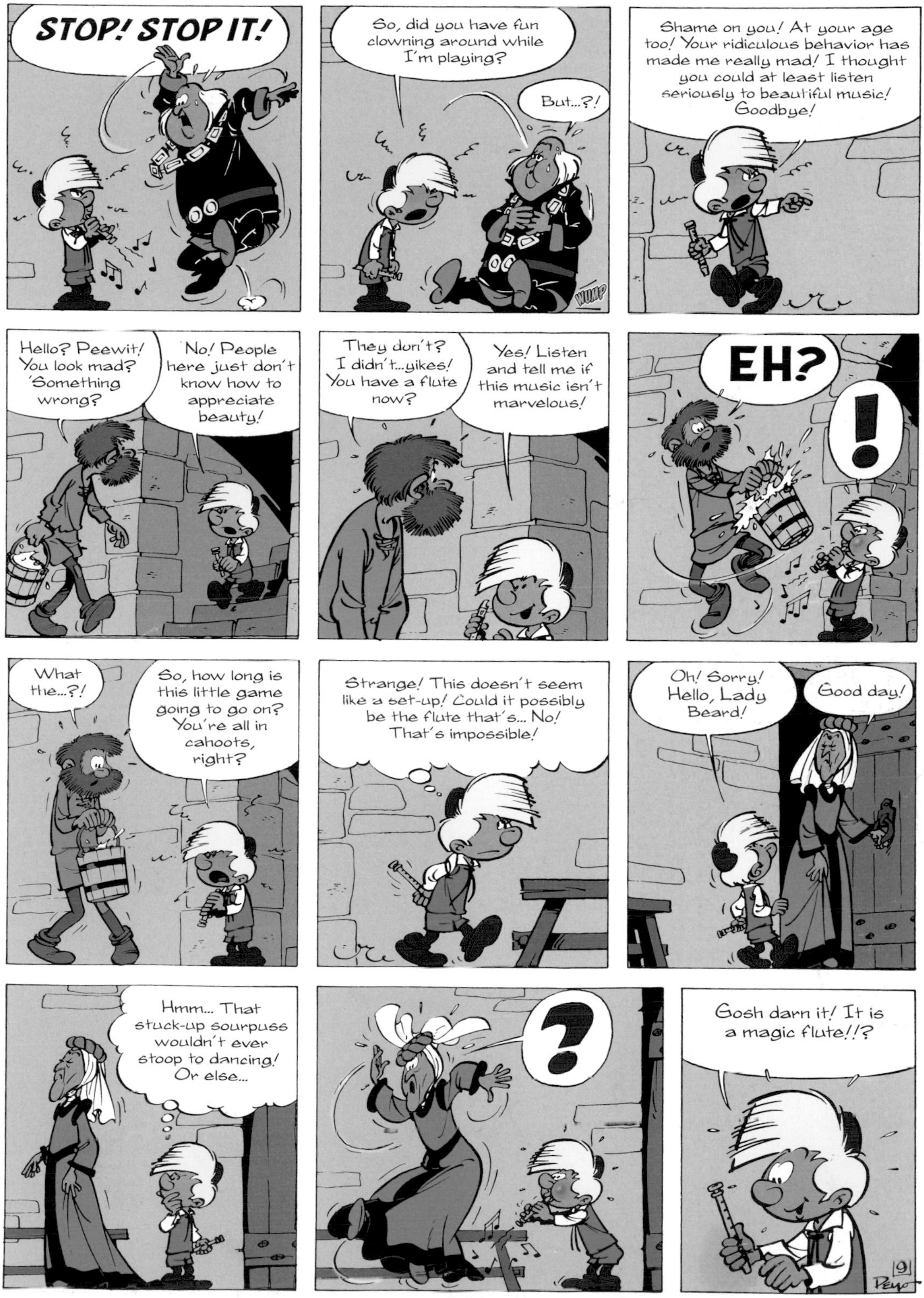
STOP! STOP IT!
So, did you have fun clowning around while I'm playing?
But...?!
WUMP
Shame on you! At your age too! Your ridiculous behavior has made me really mad! I thought you could at least listen seriously to beautiful music! Goodbye!
Hello? Peewit! You look mad? 'Something wrong?
No! People here just don't know how to appreciate beauty!
They don't? I didn't...yikes! You have a flute now?
Yes! Listen and tell me if this music isn't marvelous!
EH?
!
What the...?!
So, how long is this little game going to go on? You're all in cahoots, right?
Strange! This doesn't seem like a set-up! Could it possibly be the flute that's... No! That's impossible!
Oh! Sorry! Hello, Lady Beard!
Good day!
Hmm... That stuck-up sourpuss wouldn't ever stoop to dancing! Or else...
?
Gosh darn it! It is a magic flute!!?

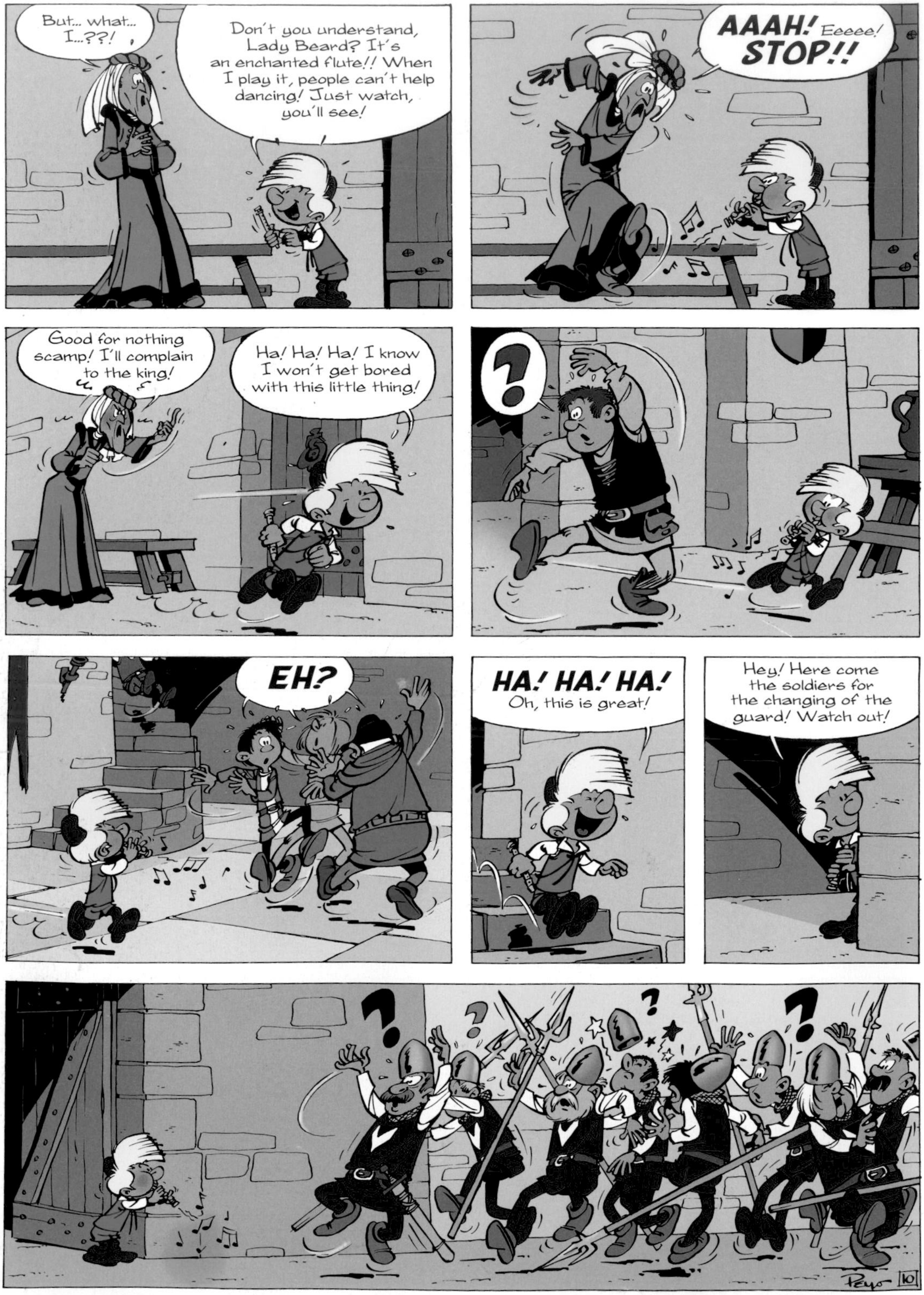
But... what... I...??!
Don't you understand, Lady Beard? It's an enchanted flute!! When I play it, people can't help dancing! Just watch, you'll see!
AAAH! Eeeee! STOP!!
Good for nothing scamp! I'll complain to the king!
Ha! Ha! Ha! I know I won't get bored with this little thing!
?
EH?
HA! HA! HA! Oh, this is great!
Hey! Here come the soldiers for the changing of the guard! Watch out!
?
?
?
Peyo 10

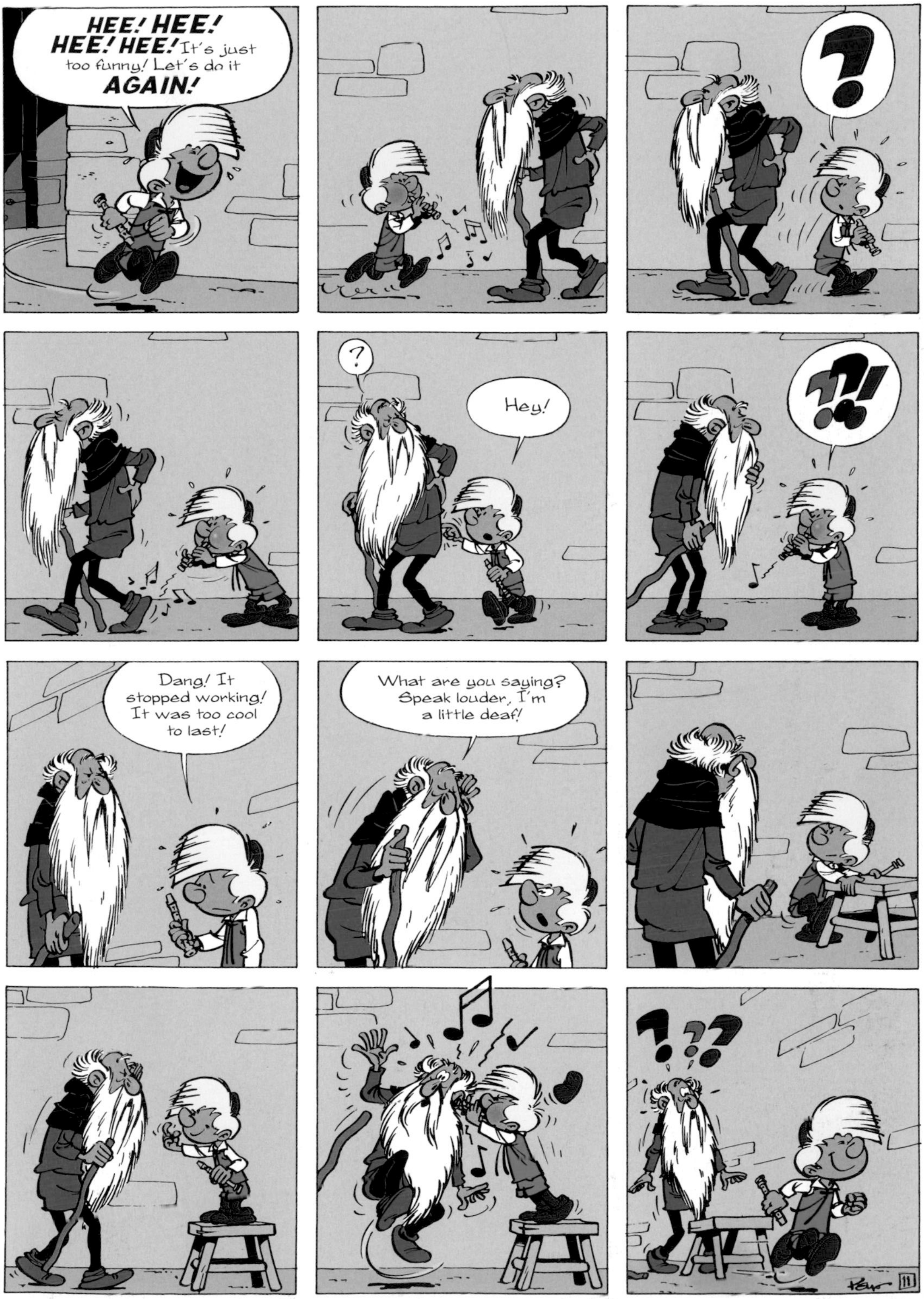
HEE! HEE! HEE! HEE! It's just too funny! Let's do it AGAIN!
?
?
Hey!
?!!
Dang! It stopped working! It was too cool to last!
What are you saying? Speak louder, I'm a little deaf!
???
11

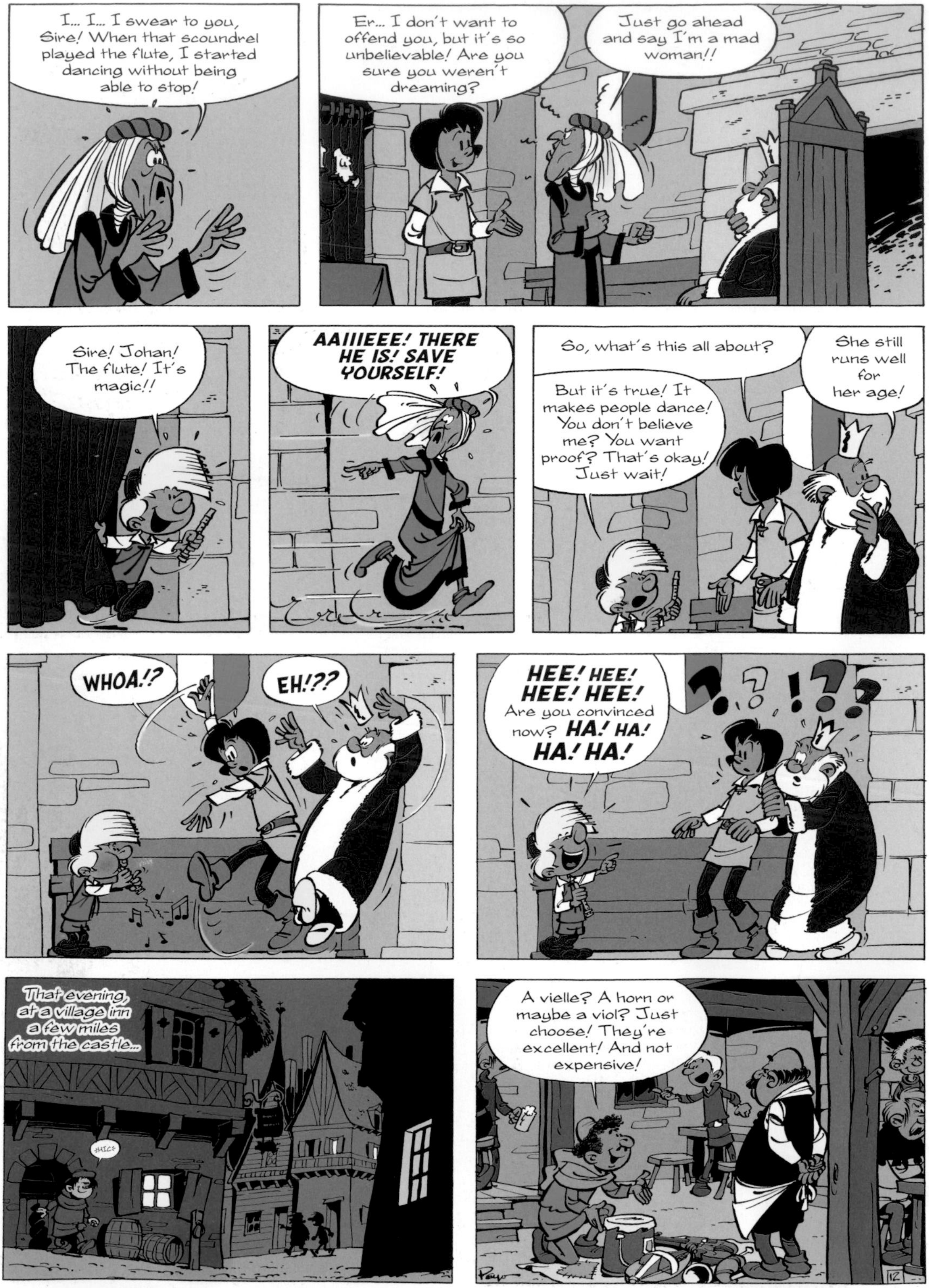
I... I... I swear to you, Sire! When that scoundrel played the flute, I started dancing without being able to stop!
Er... I don't want to offend you, but it's so unbelievable! Are you sure you weren't dreaming?
Just go ahead and say I'm a mad woman!!
Sire! Johan! The flute! It's magic!!
AAIIIEEE! THERE HE IS! SAVE YOURSELF!
So, what's this all about?
But it's true! It makes people dance! You don't believe me? You want proof? That's okay! Just wait!
She still runs well for her age!
WHOA!?
EH!??
HEE! HEE! HEE! HEE! Are you convinced now? HA! HA! HA! HA!
That evening, at a village inn a few miles from the castle...
HIC!
A vielle? A horn or maybe a viol? Just choose! They're excellent! And not expensive!

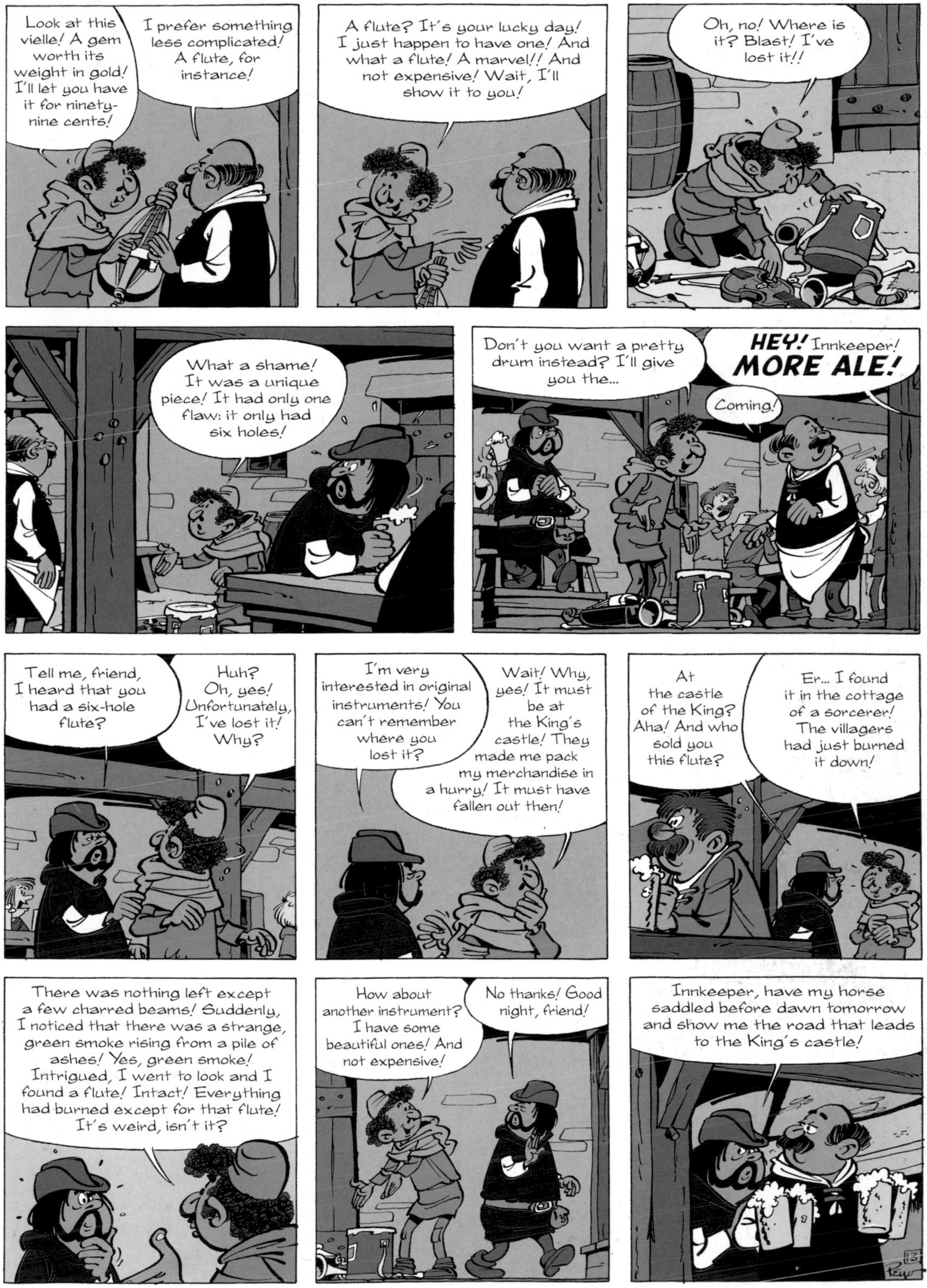
Look at this vielle! A gem worth its weight in gold! I'll let you have it for ninety-nine cents!
I prefer something less complicated! A flute, for instance!
A flute? It's your lucky day! I just happen to have one! And what a flute! A marvel!! And not expensive! Wait, I'll show it to you!
Oh, no! Where is it? Blast! I've lost it!!
What a shame! It was a unique piece! It had only one flaw: it only had six holes!
Don't you want a pretty drum instead? I'll give you the...
HEY! Innkeeper! MORE ALE!
Coming!
Tell me, friend, I heard that you had a six-hole flute?
Huh? Oh, yes! Unfortunately, I've lost it! Why?
I'm very interested in original instruments! You can't remember where you lost it?
Wait! Why, yes! It must be at the King's castle! They made me pack my merchandise in a hurry! It must have fallen out then!
At the castle of the King? Aha! And who sold you this flute?
Er... I found it in the cottage of a sorcerer! The villagers had just burned it down!
There was nothing left except a few charred beams! Suddenly, I noticed that there was a strange, green smoke rising from a pile of ashes! Yes, green smoke! Intrigued, I went to look and I found a flute! Intact! Everything had burned except for that flute! It's weird, isn't it?
How about another instrument? I have some beautiful ones! And not expensive!
No thanks! Good night, friend!
Innkeeper, have my horse saddled before dawn tomorrow and show me the road that leads to the King's castle!

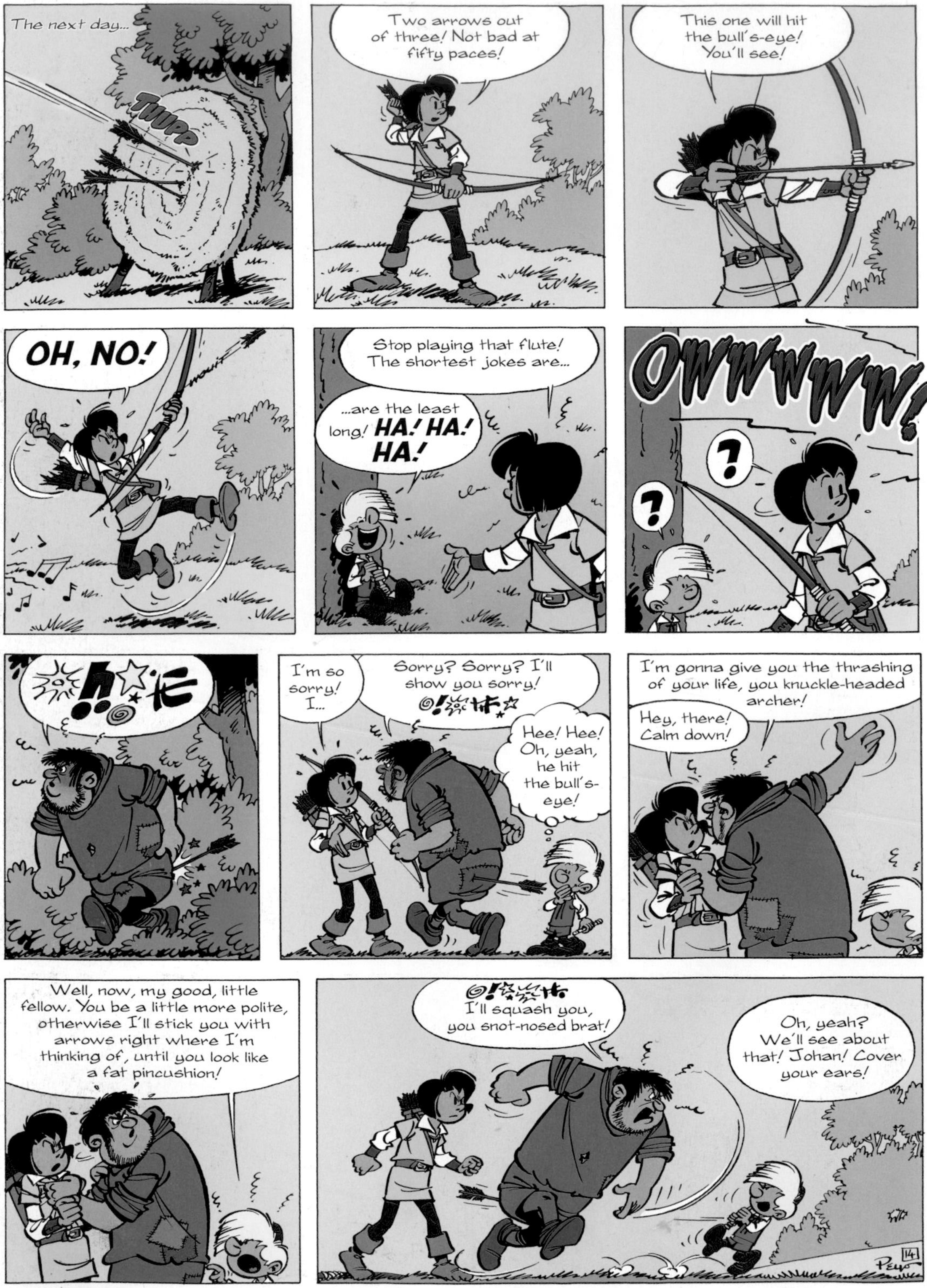
The next day...
THUPP
Two arrows out of three! Not bad at fifty paces!
This one will hit the bull's-eye! You'll see!
OH, NO!
Stop playing that flute! The shortest jokes are...
...are the least long! HA! HA! HA!
OWWWWW!
?
?
I'm so sorry! I...
Sorry? Sorry? I'll show you sorry!
Hee! Hee! Oh, yeah, he hit the bull's-eye!
I'm gonna give you the thrashing of your life, you knuckle-headed archer!
Hey, there! Calm down!
Well, now, my good, little fellow. You be a little more polite, otherwise I'll stick you with arrows right where I'm thinking of, until you look like a fat pincushion!
I'll squash you, you snot-nosed brat!
Oh, yeah? We'll see about that! Johan! Cover your ears!
14
Peyo

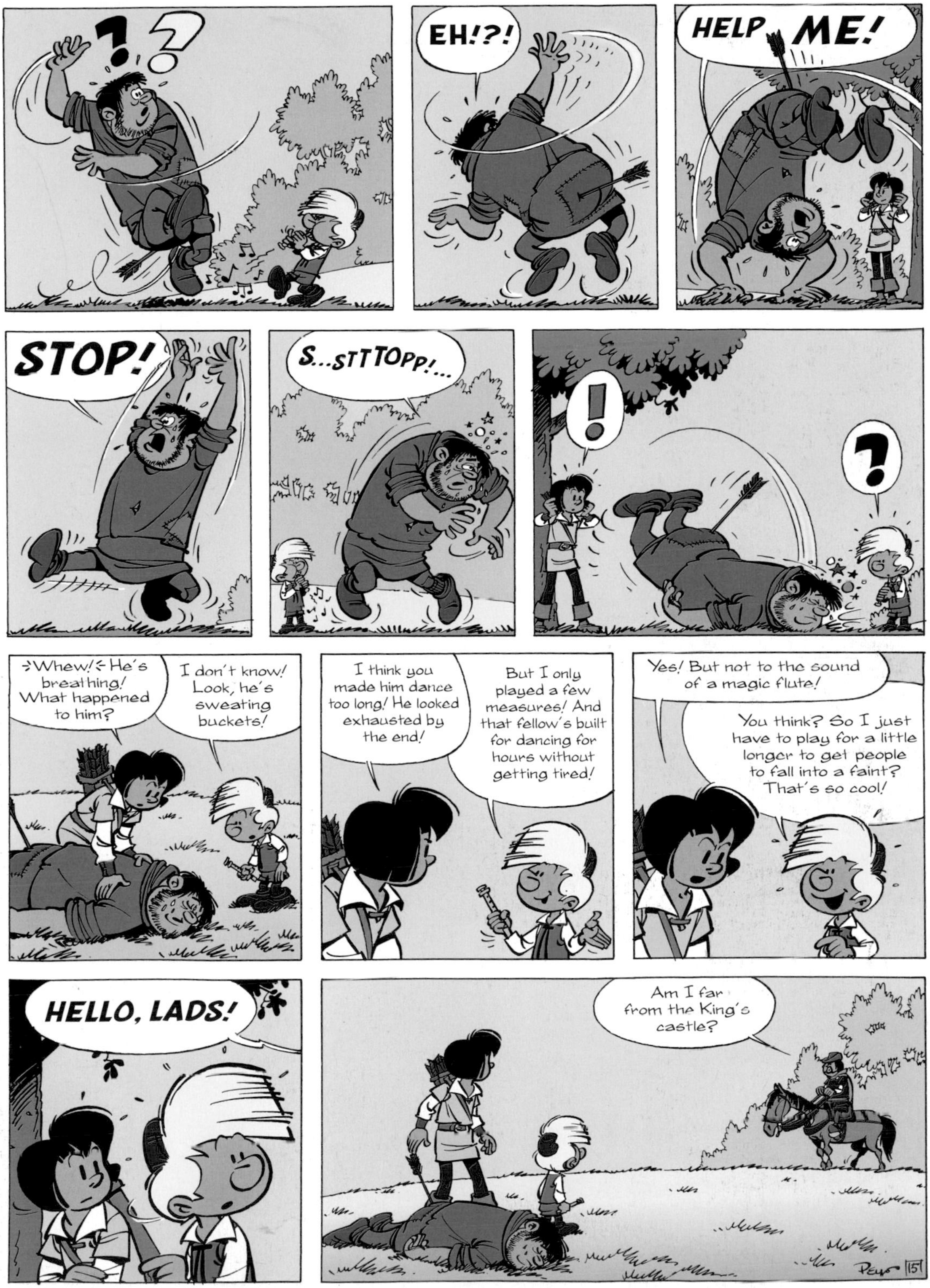
? ?
EH!?!
HELP ME!
STOP!
S...STTTOPP!...
!
?
Whew! He's breathing! What happened to him?
I don't know! Look, he's sweating buckets!
I think you made him dance too long! He looked exhausted by the end!
But I only played a few measures! And that fellow's built for dancing for hours without getting tired!
Yes! But not to the sound of a magic flute!
You think? So I just have to play for a little longer to get people to fall into a faint? That's so cool!
HELLO, LADS!
Am I far from the King's castle?
PEYO 15

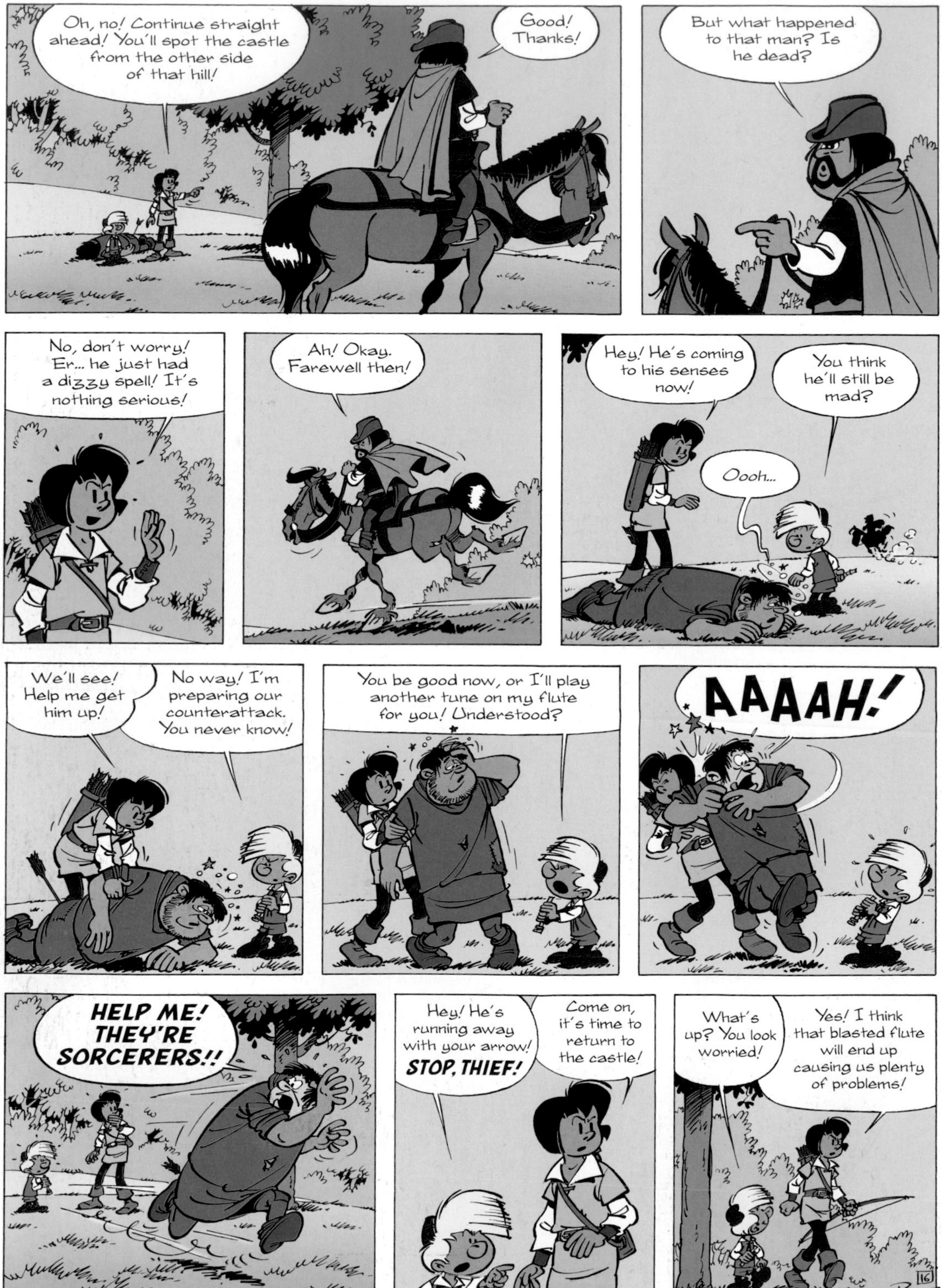
Oh, no! Continue straight ahead! You'll spot the castle from the other side of that hill!
Good! Thanks!
But what happened to that man? Is he dead?
No, don't worry! Er... he just had a dizzy spell! It's nothing serious!
Ah! Okay. Farewell then!
Hey! He's coming to his senses now!
You think he'll still be mad?
Oooh...
We'll see! Help me get him up!
No way! I'm preparing our counterattack. You never know!
You be good now, or I'll play another tune on my flute for you! Understood?
AAAAH!
HELP ME! THEY'RE SORCERERS!!
Hey! He's running away with your arrow! STOP, THIEF!
Come on, it's time to return to the castle!
What's up? You look worried!
Yes! I think that blasted flute will end up causing us plenty of problems!
16
PEYO

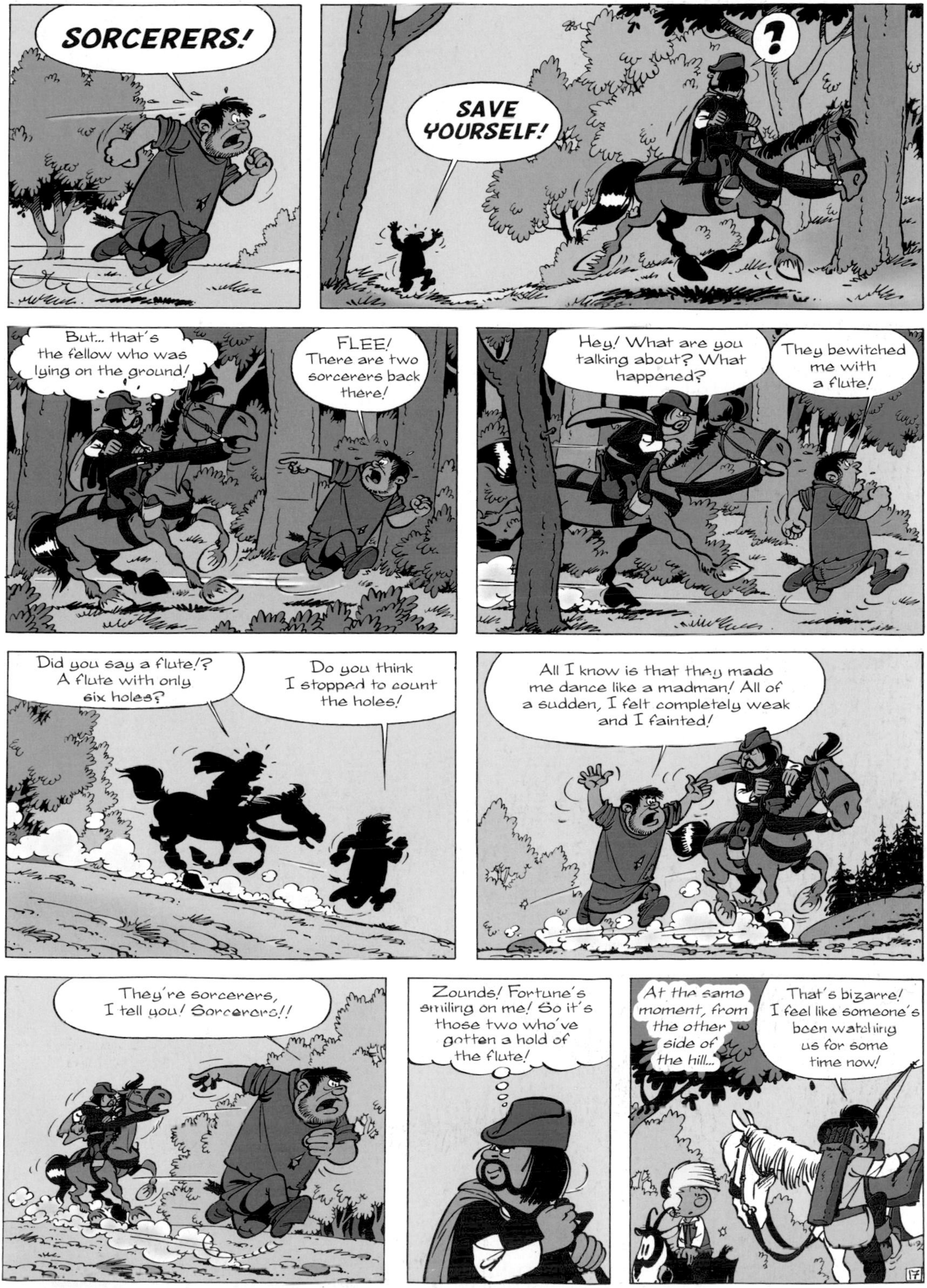
SORCERERS!
SAVE YOURSELF!
?
But... that's the fellow who was lying on the ground!
FLEE! There are two sorcerers back there!
Hey! What are you talking about? What happened?
They bewitched me with a flute!
Did you say a flute!? A flute with only six holes?
Do you think I stopped to count the holes!
All I know is that they made me dance like a madman! All of a sudden, I felt completely weak and I fainted!
They're sorcerers, I tell you! Sorcerers!!
Zounds! Fortune's smiling on me! So it's those two who've gotten a hold of the flute!
At the same moment, from the other side of the hill...
That's bizarre! I feel like someone's been watching us for some time now!
17

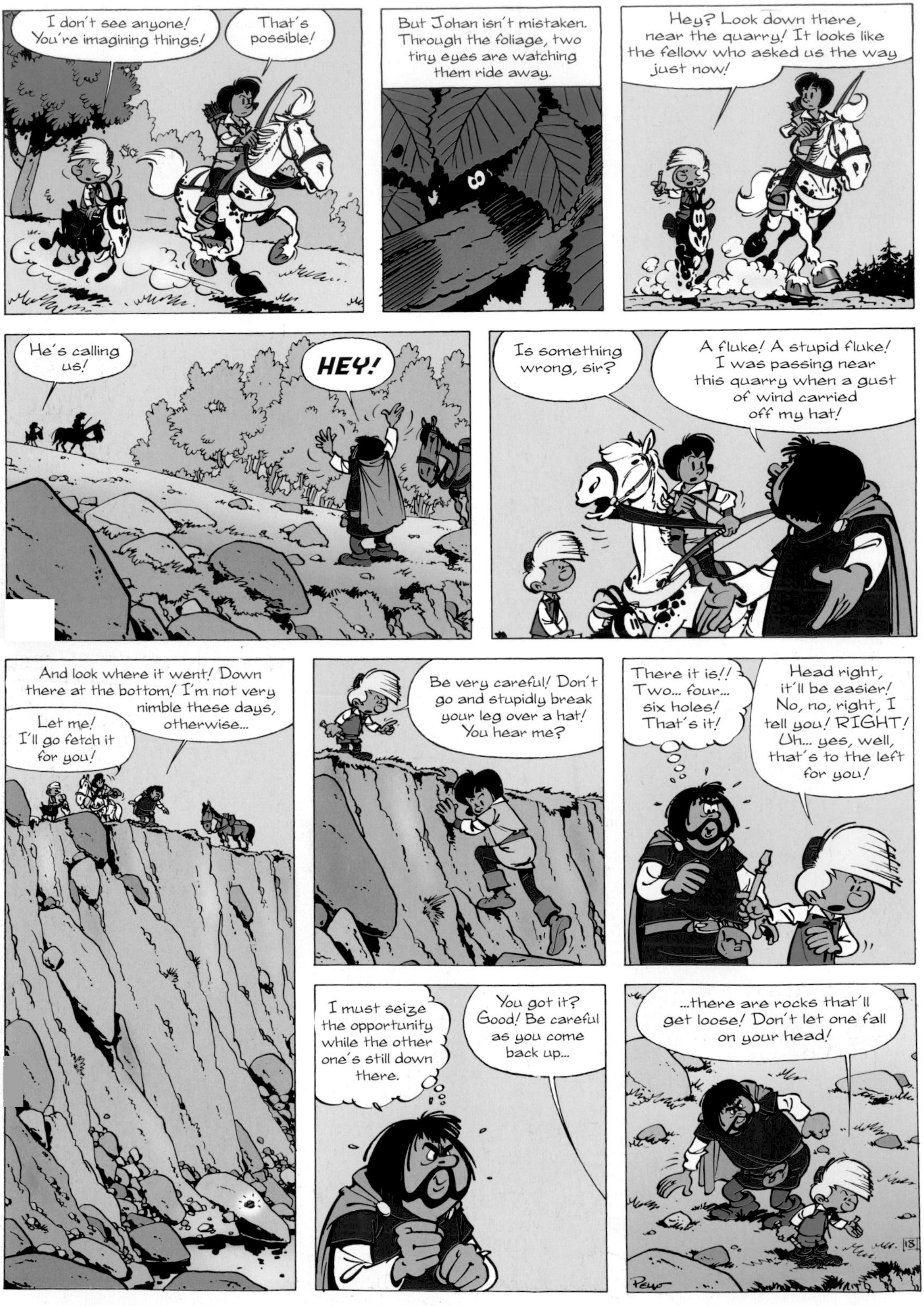

I don't see anyone! You're imagining things!
That's possible!
But Johan isn't mistaken. Through the foliage, two tiny eyes are watching them ride away.
Hey? Look down there, near the quarry! It looks like the fellow who asked us the way just now!
He's calling us!
HEY!
Is something wrong, sir?
A fluke! A stupid fluke! I was passing near this quarry when a gust of wind carried off my hat!
And look where it went! Down there at the bottom! I'm not very nimble these days, otherwise...
Let me! I'll go fetch it for you!
Be very careful! Don't go and stupidly break your leg over a hat! You hear me?
There it is!! Two... four... six holes! That's it!
Head right, it'll be easier! No, no, right, I tell you! RIGHT! Uh... yes, well, that's to the left for you!
I must seize the opportunity while the other one's still down there.
You got it? Good! Be careful as you come back up...
...there are rocks that'll get loose! Don't let one fall on your head!
18

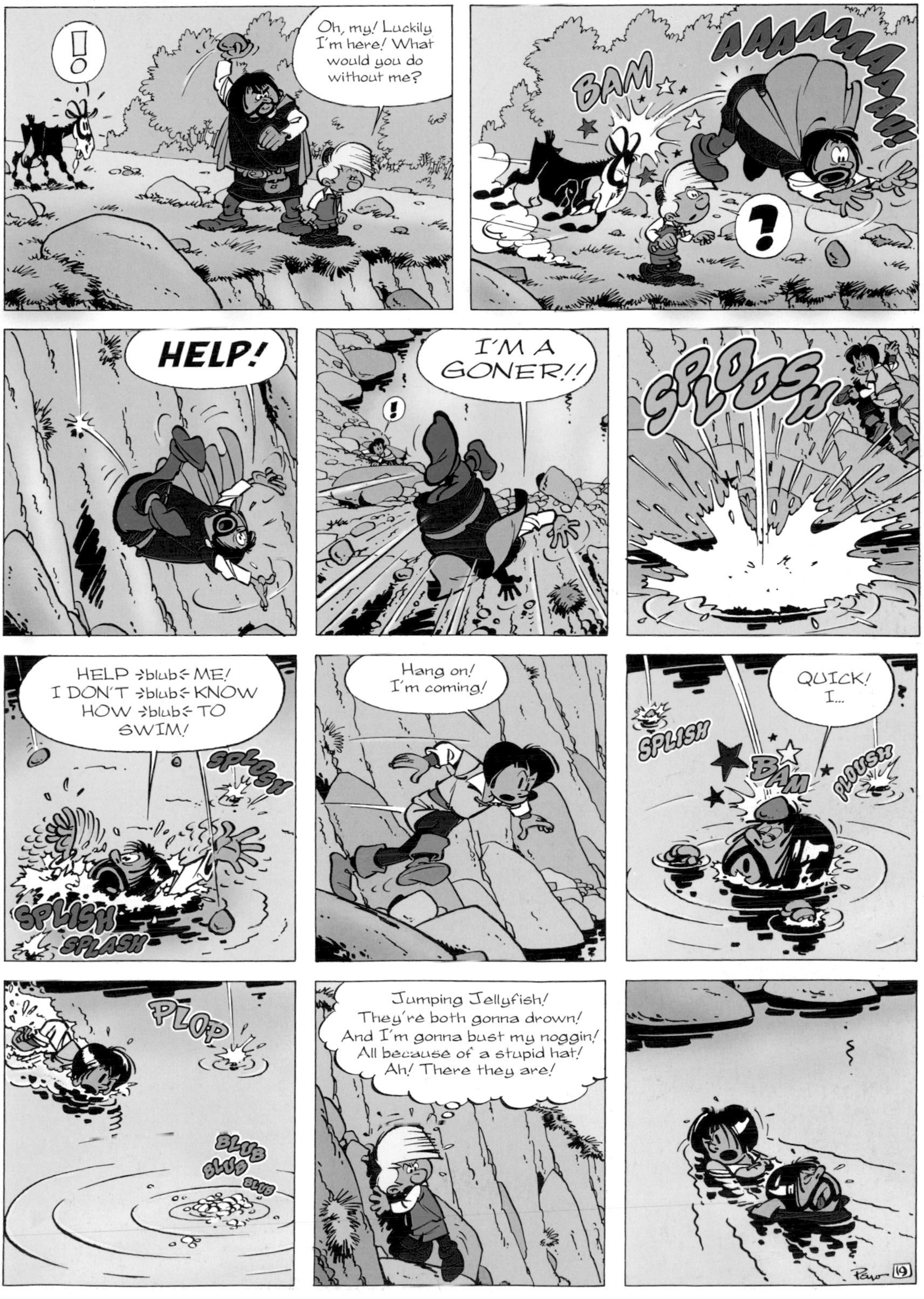
!?
Oh, my! Luckily I'm here! What would you do without me?
BAM
AAAAAAAAAAH!!
?
HELP!
!
I'M A GONER!!
SPLOOSH
HELP -blub- ME! I DON'T -blub- KNOW HOW -blub- TO SWIM!
SPLOSH
SPLISH
SPLASH
Hang on! I'm coming!
SPLISH
QUICK! I...
BAM
PLOUSH
PLOP
BLUB
BLUB
BLUB
Jumping Jellyfish! They're both gonna drown! And I'm gonna bust my noggin! All because of a stupid hat! Ah! There they are!
19

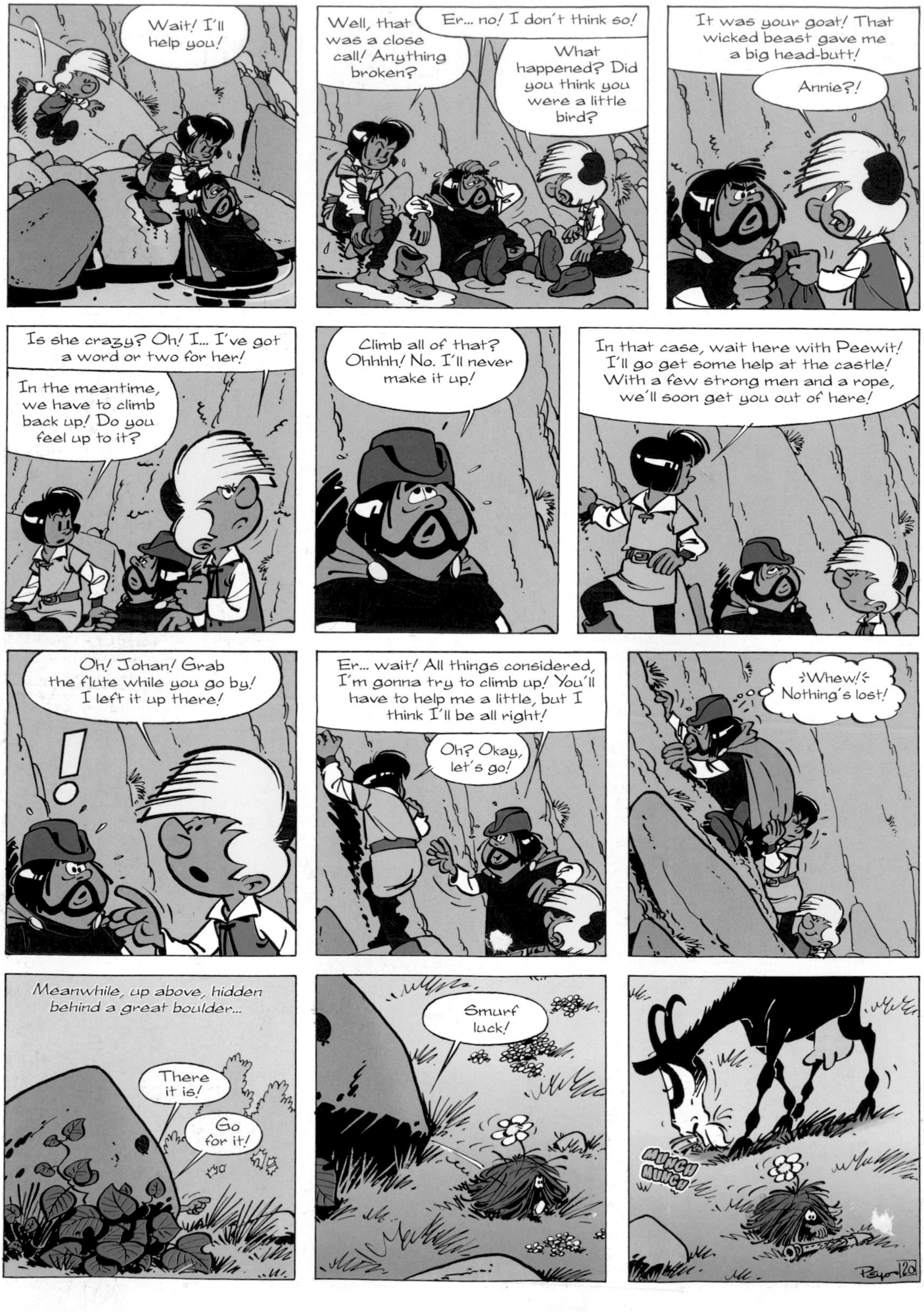

Wait! I'll help you!
Well, that was a close call! Anything broken?
Er... no! I don't think so!
What happened? Did you think you were a little bird?
It was your goat! That wicked beast gave me a big head-butt!
Annie?!
Is she crazy? Oh! I... I've got a word or two for her!
In the meantime, we have to climb back up! Do you feel up to it?
Climb all of that? Ohhhh! No. I'll never make it up!
In that case, wait here with Peewit! I'll go get some help at the castle! With a few strong men and a rope, we'll soon get you out of here!
!
Oh! Johan! Grab the flute while you go by! I left it up there!
Er... wait! All things considered, I'm gonna try to climb up! You'll have to help me a little, but I think I'll be all right!
Oh? Okay, let's go!
Whew! Nothing's lost!
Meanwhile, up above, hidden behind a great boulder...
There it is!
Go for it!
Smurf luck!
MUNCH MUNCH
Peyo
20

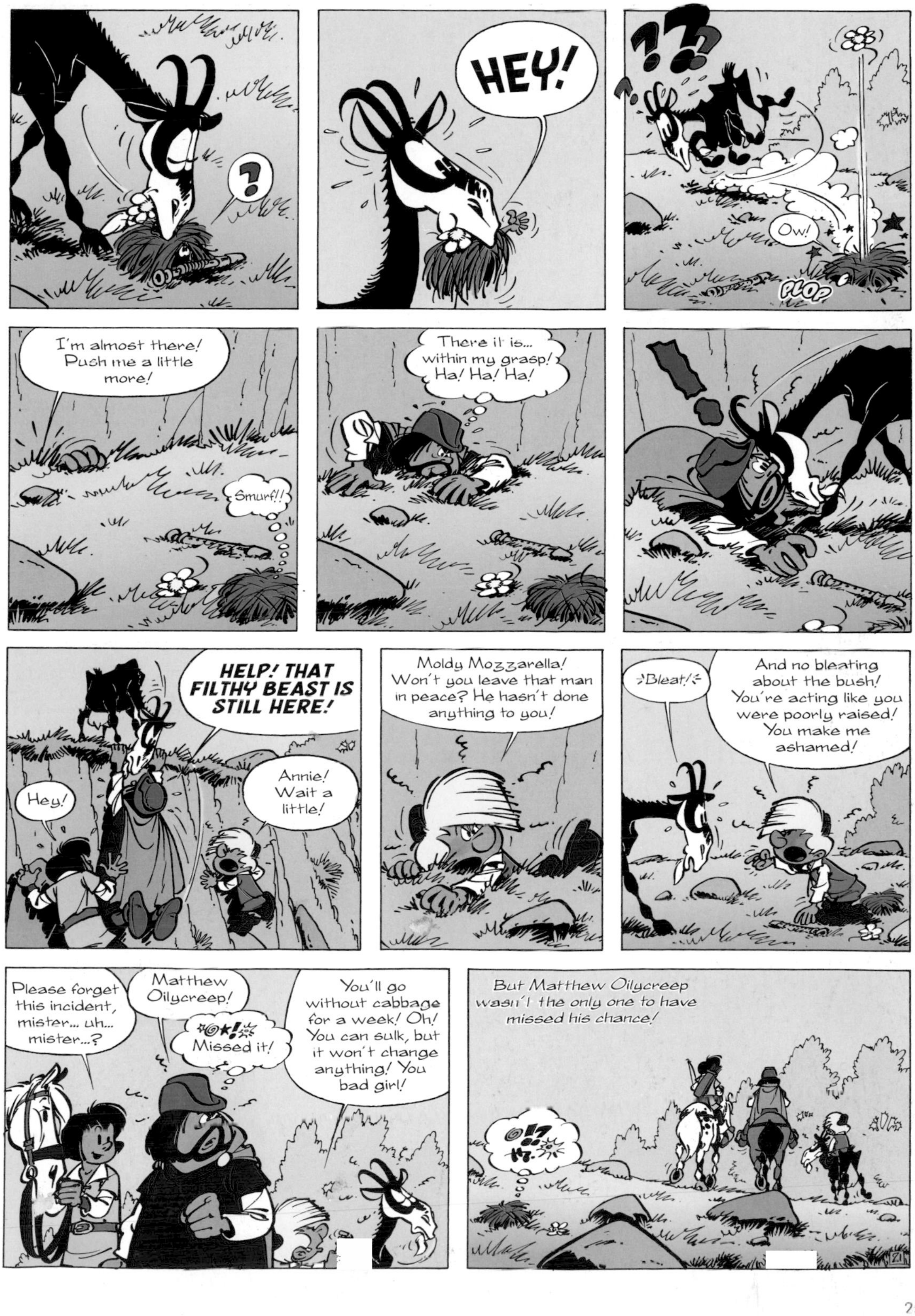
?
HEY!
??
Ow!
PLOP
I'm almost there! Push me a little more!
Smurf!!
There it is... within my grasp! Ha! Ha! Ha!
HELP! THAT FILTHY BEAST IS STILL HERE!
Hey!
Annie! Wait a little!
Moldy Mozzarella! Won't you leave that man in peace? He hasn't done anything to you!
Bleat!
And no bleating about the bush! You're acting like you were poorly raised! You make me ashamed!
Please forget this incident, mister... uh... mister...?
Matthew Oilycreep!
Missed it!
You'll go without cabbage for a week! Oh! You can sulk, but it won't change anything! You bad girl!
But Matthew Oilycreep wasn't the only one to have missed his chance!

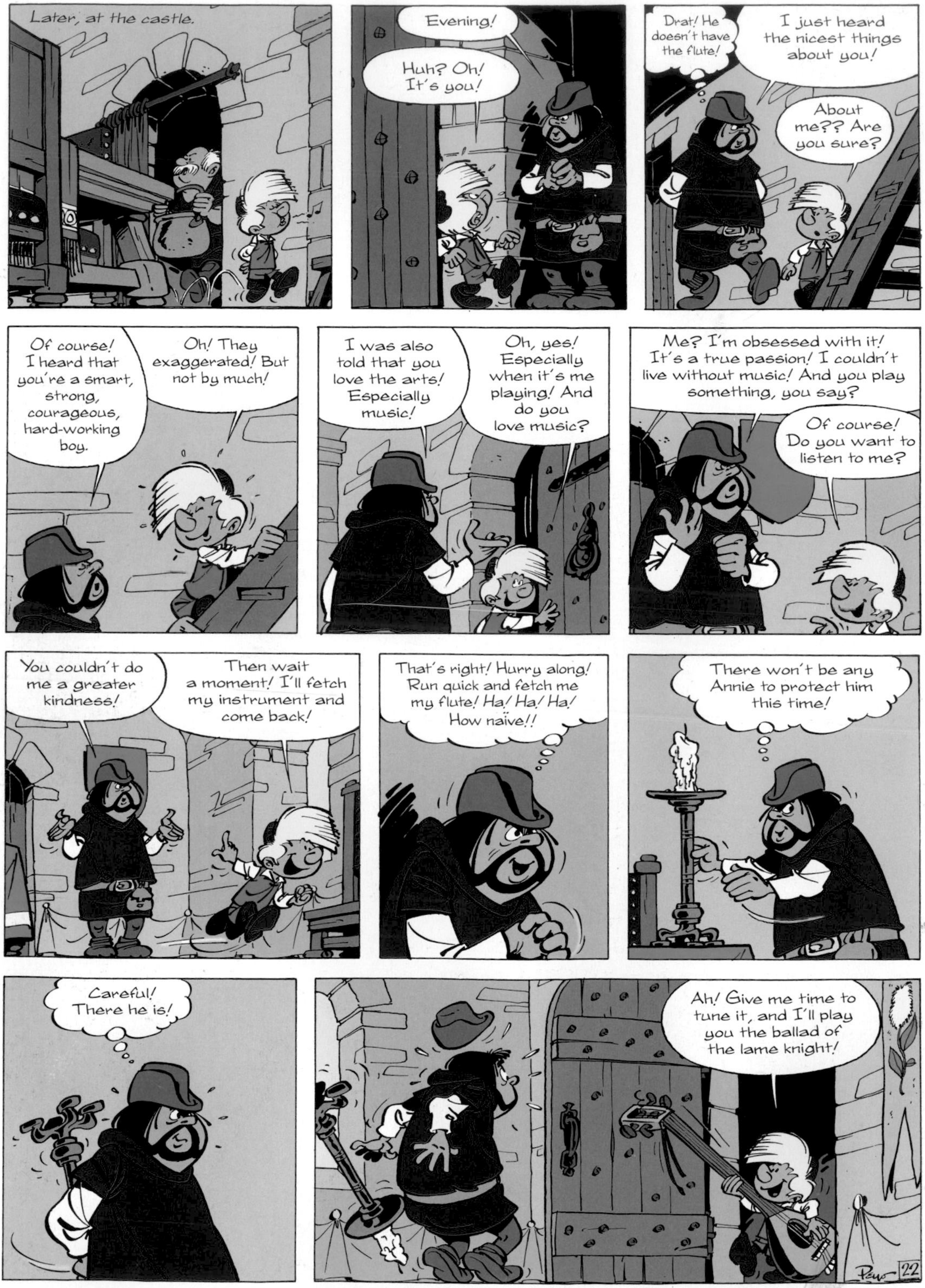
Later, at the castle.
Evening!
Huh? Oh! It's you!
Drat! He doesn't have the flute!
I just heard the nicest things about you!
About me?? Are you sure?
Of course! I heard that you're a smart, strong, courageous, hard-working boy.
Oh! They exaggerated! But not by much!
I was also told that you love the arts! Especially music!
Oh, yes! Especially when it's me playing! And do you love music?
Me? I'm obsessed with it! It's a true passion! I couldn't live without music! And you play something, you say?
Of course! Do you want to listen to me?
You couldn't do me a greater kindness!
Then wait a moment! I'll fetch my instrument and come back!
That's right! Hurry along! Run quick and fetch me my flute! Ha! Ha! Ha! How naïve!!
There won't be any Annie to protect him this time!
Careful! There he is!
Ah! Give me time to tune it, and I'll play you the ballad of the lame knight!
Peyo 22

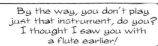
Two hours later...

ALL MY SERV-ICE YOU OWE ME. TO-DAY, PLEASE, RETURN TO ME.

Beautiful, eh? Should I sing you another song?

NO! NO!! It was splendid, magnificent, but, er... you mustn't overdo good things!

By the way, you don't play just that instrument, do you? I thought I saw you with a flute earlier!

Yes! Only, I'd just like to warn you that it's not an ordinary flute!

It's a MAGIC flute! When I play it, people start dancing without being able to stop!

Ha! Ha! Ha! You don't really expect me to believe that! A magic flute! Why, that doesn't exist!

It doesn't? Well, come with me! I'll show you whether or not it exists!

I'll get it this time!

Don't come complaining to me if I make you dance like a cat on a hot tin roof! You're the one who asked for it!

DING DONG

Oh! Listen!

What? What is it?

DING DONG DING DONG DING !

WOOHOO! That's the bell for the evening meal! Yum yum! Come quick!

But @!?¤☼ will I ★¤†✿⊙ ever end up getting that ✵☆ flute one day??!

27

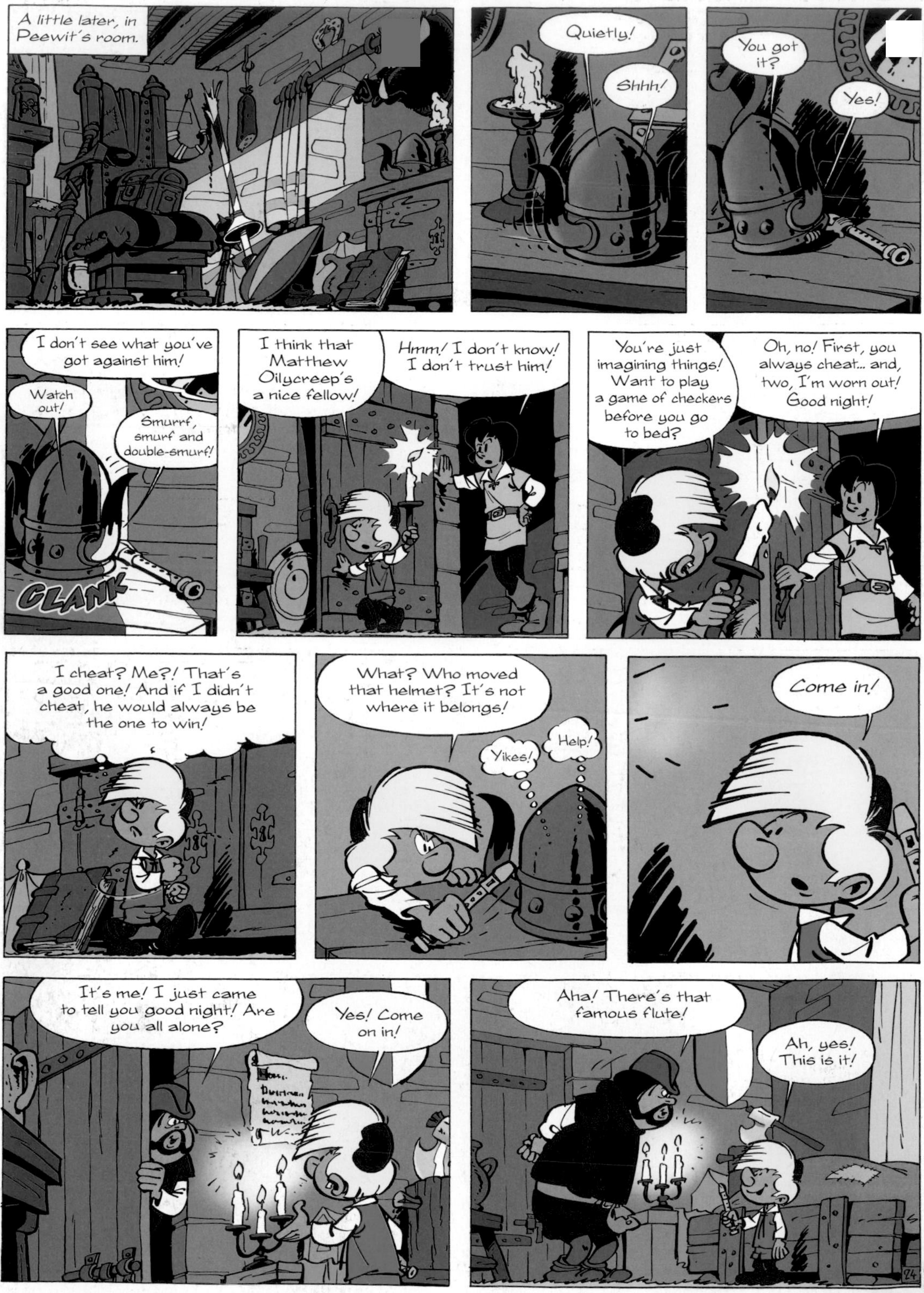
A little later, in Peewit's room.
Quietly!
Shhh!
You got it?
Yes!
I don't see what you've got against him!
Watch out!
Smurf, smurf and double-smurf!
CLANK
I think that Matthew Oilycreep's a nice fellow!
Hmm! I don't know! I don't trust him!
You're just imagining things! Want to play a game of checkers before you go to bed?
Oh, no! First, you always cheat... and, two, I'm worn out! Good night!
I cheat? Me?! That's a good one! And if I didn't cheat, he would always be the one to win!
What? Who moved that helmet? It's not where it belongs!
Yikes!
Help!
Come in!
It's me! I just came to tell you good night! Are you all alone?
Yes! Come on in!
Aha! There's that famous flute!
Ah, yes! This is it!

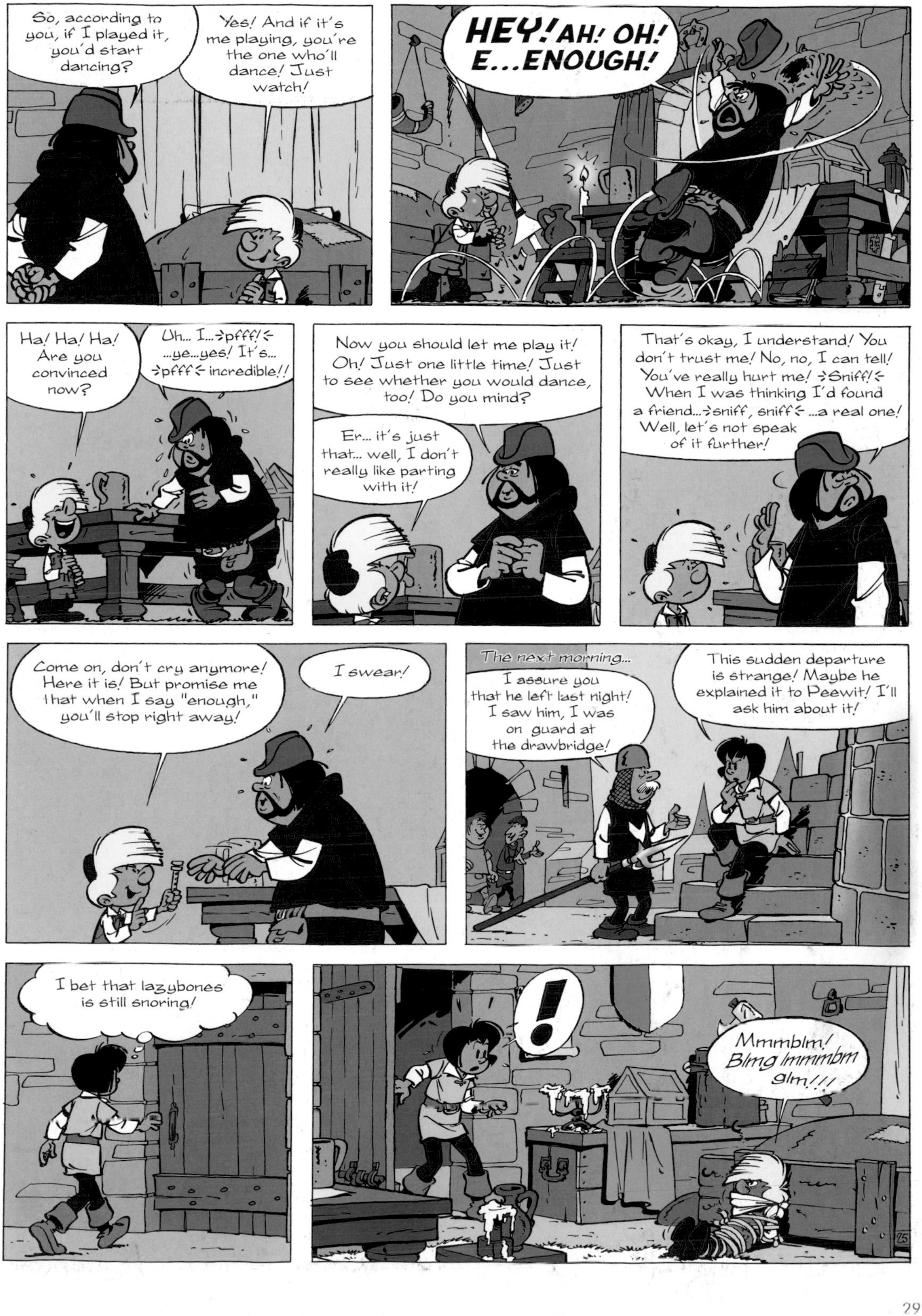

So, according to you, if I played it, you'd start dancing?
Yes! And if it's me playing, you're the one who'll dance! Just watch!
HEY! AH! OH! E...ENOUGH!
Ha! Ha! Ha! Are you convinced now?
Uh... I...›pfff!‹ ...ye...yes! It's... ›pfff‹ incredible!!
Now you should let me play it! Oh! Just one little time! Just to see whether you would dance, too! Do you mind?
Er... it's just that... well, I don't really like parting with it!
That's okay, I understand! You don't trust me! No, no, I can tell! You've really hurt me! ›Sniff!‹ When I was thinking I'd found a friend...›sniff, sniff‹ ...a real one! Well, let's not speak of it further!
Come on, don't cry anymore! Here it is! But promise me that when I say "enough," you'll stop right away!
I swear!
The next morning...
I assure you that he left last night! I saw him, I was on guard at the drawbridge!
This sudden departure is strange! Maybe he explained it to Peewit! I'll ask him about it!
I bet that lazybones is still snoring!
!
Mmmblm! Blmg lmmmbm glm!!!

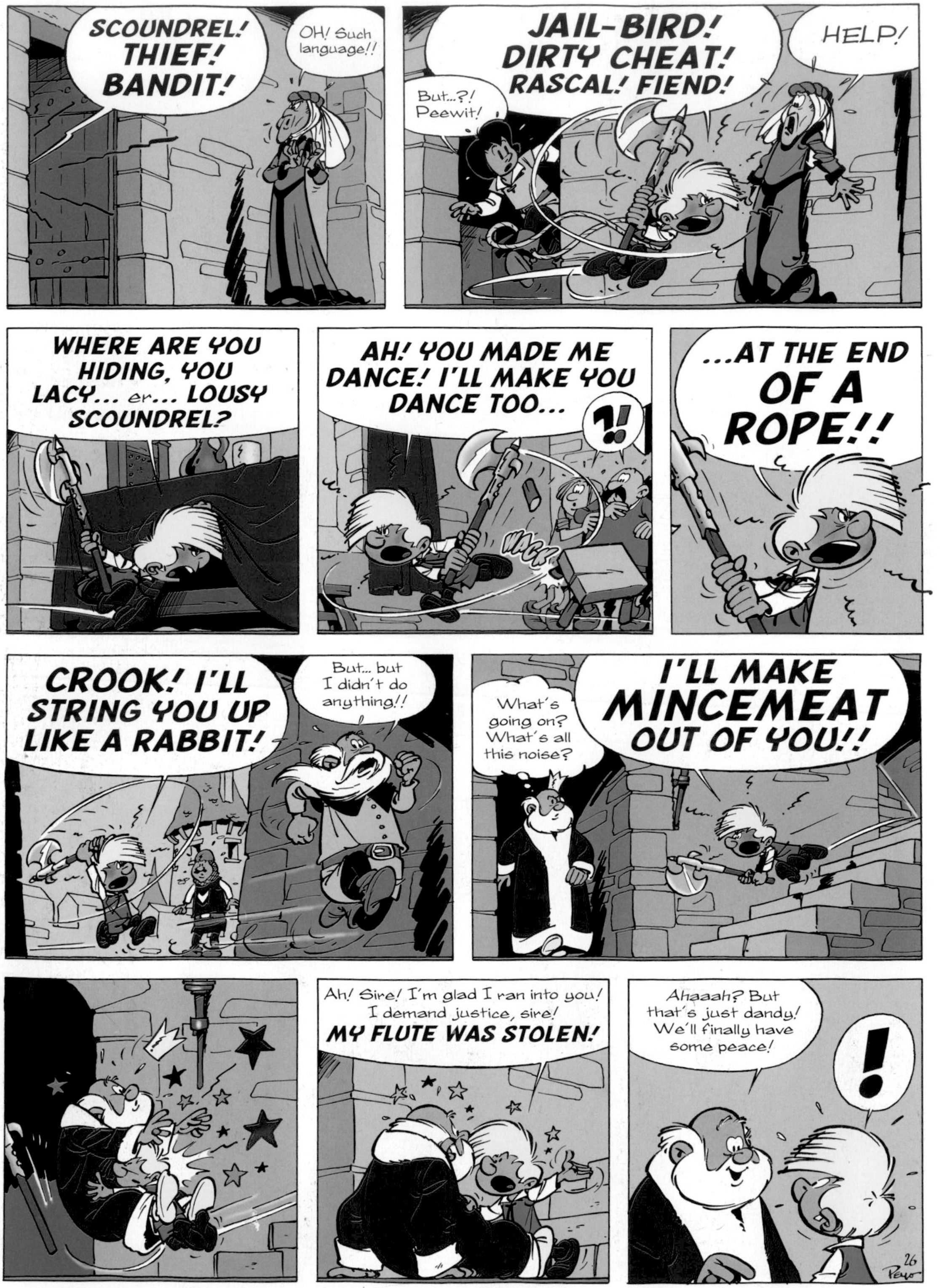
SCOUNDREL! THIEF! BANDIT!
OH! Such language!!
JAIL-BIRD! DIRTY CHEAT! RASCAL! FIEND!
HELP!
But...?! Peewit!
WHERE ARE YOU HIDING, YOU LACY... er... LOUSY SCOUNDREL?
AH! YOU MADE ME DANCE! I'LL MAKE YOU DANCE TOO...
?!!
...AT THE END OF A ROPE!!
CROOK! I'LL STRING YOU UP LIKE A RABBIT!
But... but I didn't do anything!!
What's going on? What's all this noise?
I'LL MAKE MINCEMEAT OUT OF YOU!!
Ah! Sire! I'm glad I ran into you! I demand justice, sire! MY FLUTE WAS STOLEN!
Ahaaah? But that's just dandy! We'll finally have some peace!
!
26

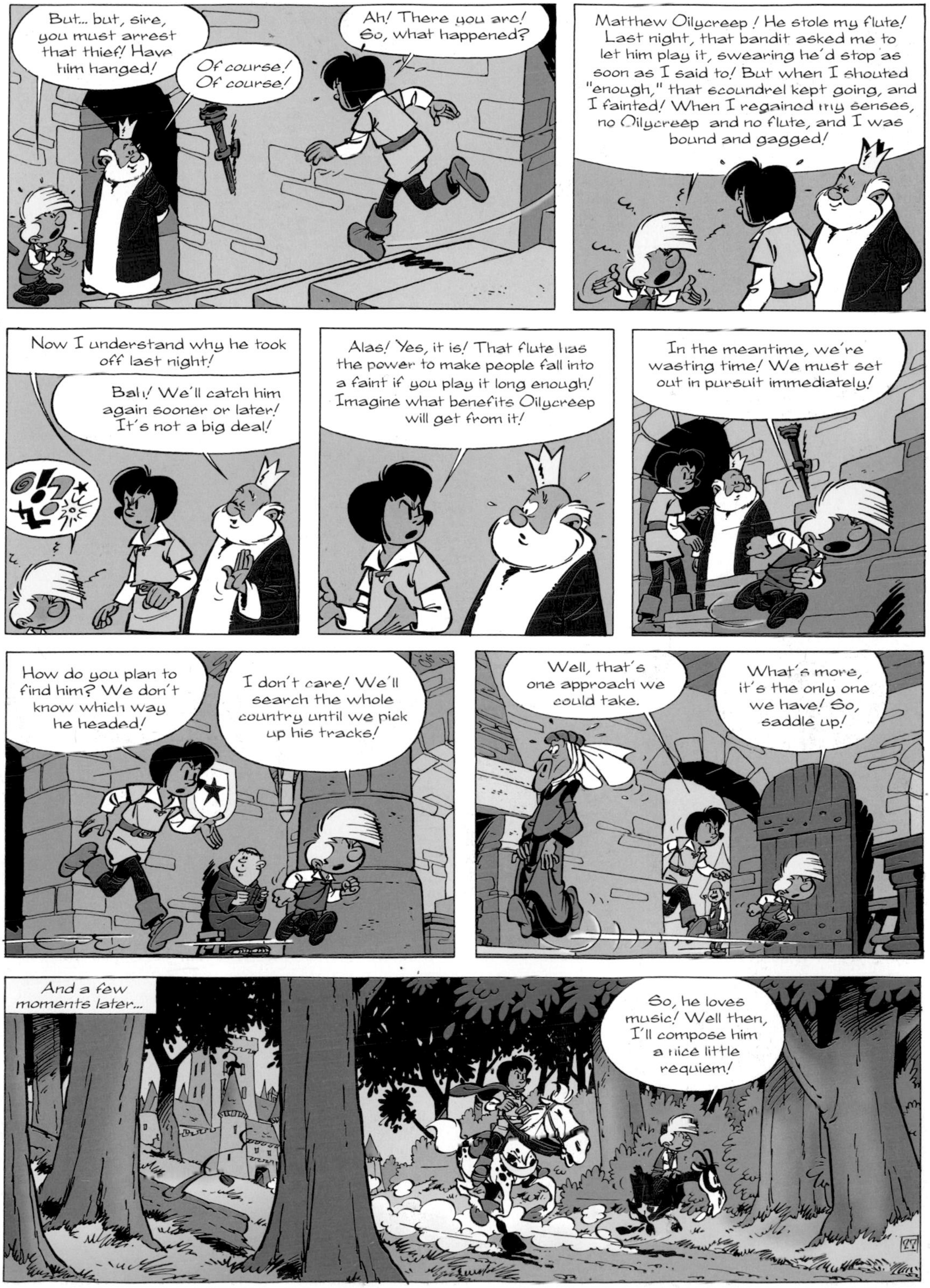
But... but, sire, you must arrest that thief! Hava him hanged!
Of course! Of course!
Ah! There you are! So, what happened?
Matthew Oilycreep ! He stole my flute! Last night, that bandit asked me to let him play it, swearing he'd stop as soon as I said to! But when I shouted "enough," that scoundrel kept going, and I fainted! When I regained my senses, no Oilycreep and no flute, and I was bound and gagged!
Now I understand why he took off last night!
Bah! We'll catch him again sooner or later! It's not a big deal!
Alas! Yes, it is! That flute has the power to make people fall into a faint if you play it long enough! Imagine what benefits Oilycreep will get from it!
In the meantime, we're wasting time! We must set out in pursuit immediately!
How do you plan to find him? We don't know which way he headed!
I don't care! We'll search the whole country until we pick up his tracks!
Well, that's one approach we could take.
What's more, it's the only one we have! So, saddle up!
And a few moments later...
So, he loves music! Well then, I'll compose him a nice little requiem!

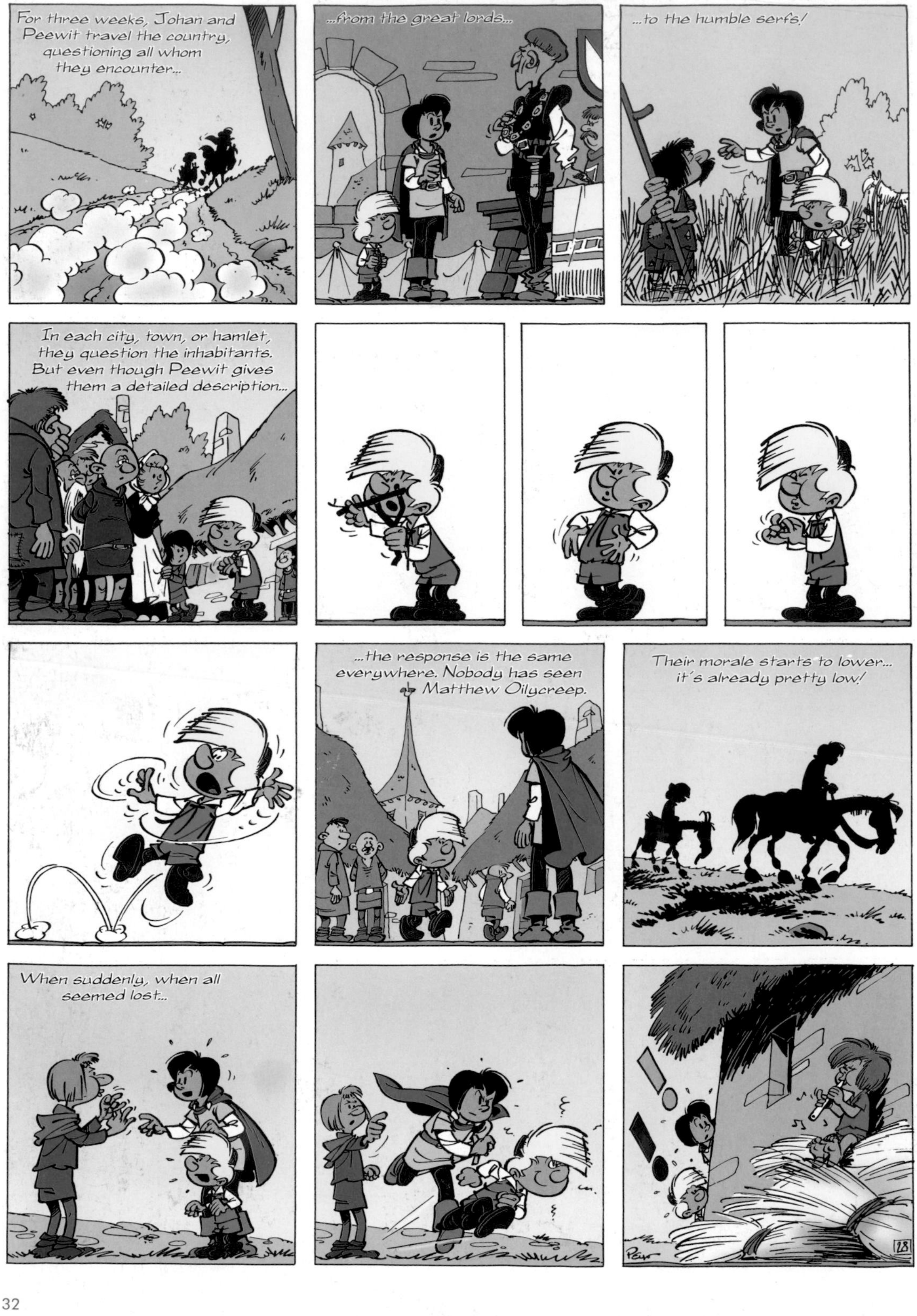

For three weeks, Johan and Peewit travel the country, questioning all whom they encounter...
...from the great lords...
...to the humble serfs!
In each city, town, or hamlet, they question the inhabitants. But even though Peewit gives them a detailed description...
...the response is the same everywhere. Nobody has seen Matthew Oilycreep.
Their morale starts to lower... it's already pretty low!
When suddenly, when all seemed lost...
28

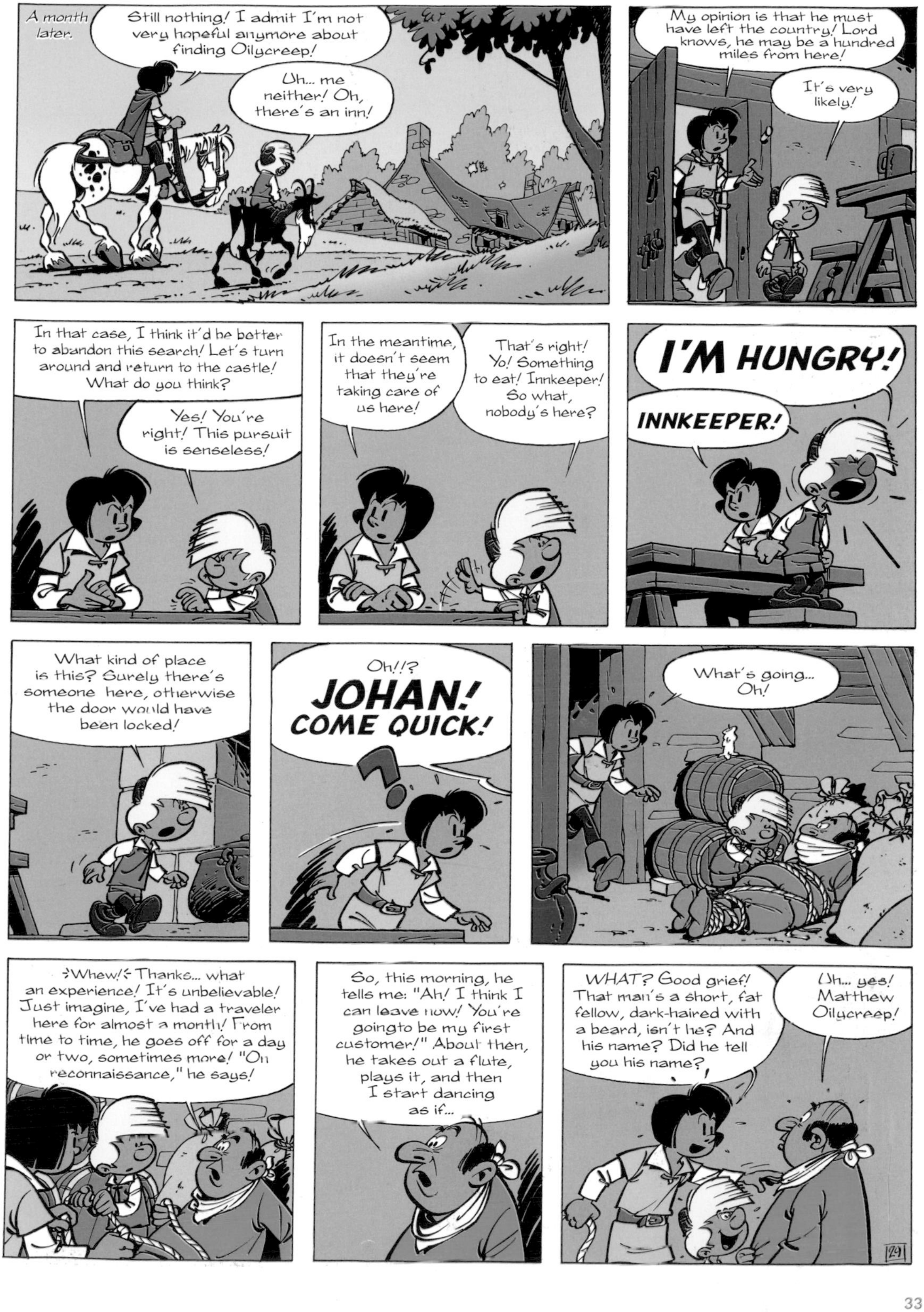
A month later.
Still nothing! I admit I'm not very hopeful anymore about finding Oilycreep!
Uh... me neither! Oh, there's an inn!
My opinion is that he must have left the country! Lord knows, he may be a hundred miles from here!
It's very likely!
In that case, I think it'd be better to abandon this search! Let's turn around and return to the castle! What do you think?
Yes! You're right! This pursuit is senseless!
In the meantime, it doesn't seem that they're taking care of us here!
That's right! Yo! Something to eat! Innkeeper! So what, nobody's here?
I'M HUNGRY!
INNKEEPER!
What kind of place is this? Surely there's someone here, otherwise the door would have been locked!
Oh!!?
JOHAN! COME QUICK!
What's going... Oh!
Whew! Thanks... what an experience! It's unbelievable! Just imagine, I've had a traveler here for almost a month! From time to time, he goes off for a day or two, sometimes more! "On reconnaissance," he says!
So, this morning, he tells me: "Ah! I think I can leave now! You're goingto be my first customer!" About then, he takes out a flute, plays it, and then I start dancing as if...
WHAT? Good grief! That man's a short, fat fellow, dark-haired with a beard, isn't he? And his name? Did he tell you his name?
Uh... yes! Matthew Oilycreep!
29

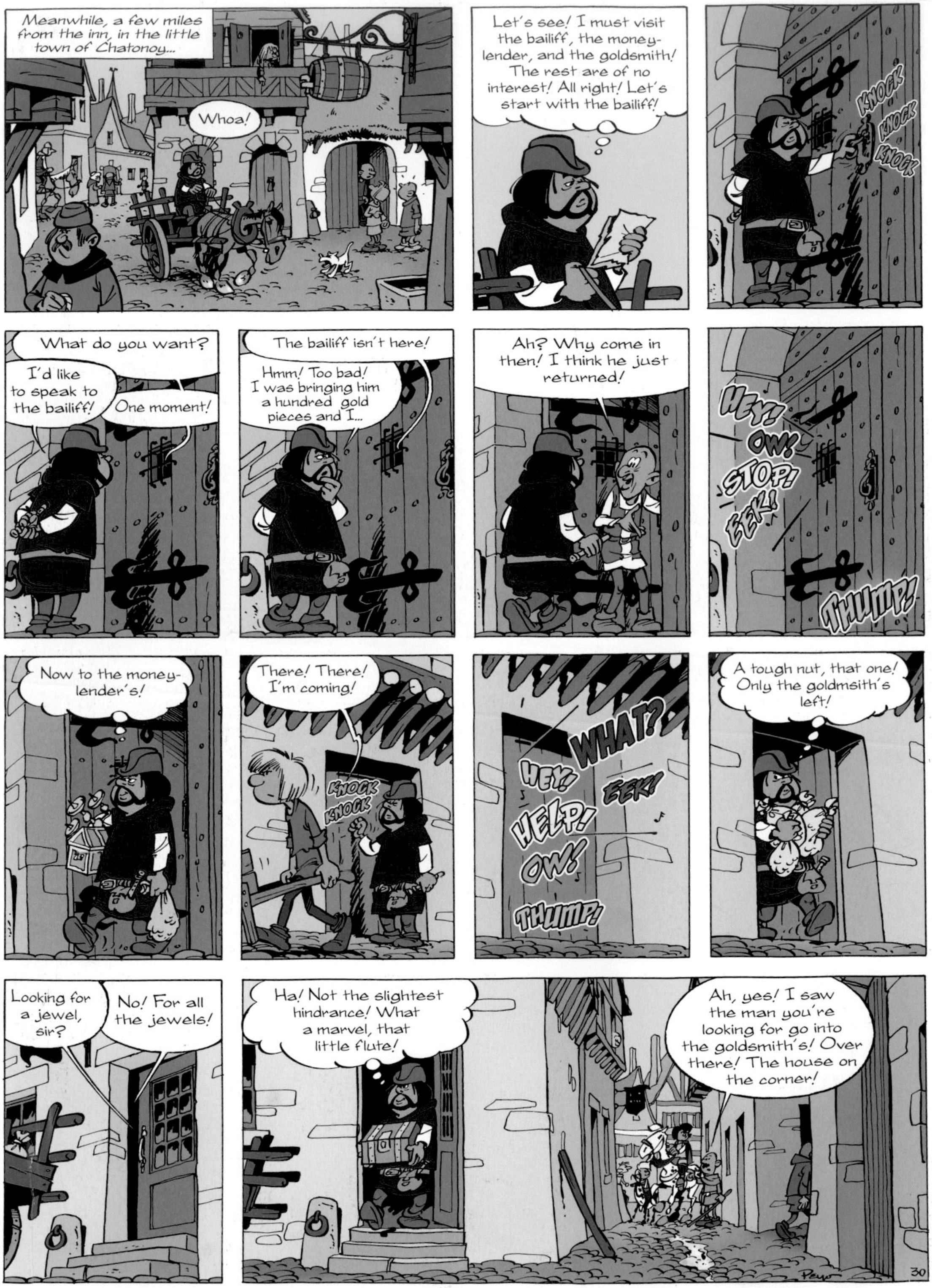
Meanwhile, a few miles from the inn, in the little town of Chatonoy...
Whoa!
Let's see! I must visit the bailiff, the money-lender, and the goldsmith! The rest are of no interest! All right! Let's start with the bailiff!
KNOCK
KNOCK
KNOCK
What do you want?
I'd like to speak to the bailiff!
One moment!
The bailiff isn't here!
Hmm! Too bad! I was bringing him a hundred gold pieces and I...
Ah? Why come in then! I think he just returned!
HEY!
OW!
STOP!
EEK!
THUMP!
Now to the money-lender's!
There! There! I'm coming!
KNOCK
KNOCK
WHAT?
HEY!
EEK!
HELP!
OW!
THUMP!
A tough nut, that one! Only the goldsmith's left!
Looking for a jewel, sir?
No! For all the jewels!
Ha! Not the slightest hindrance! What a marvel, that little flute!
Ah, yes! I saw the man you're looking for go into the goldsmith's! Over there! The house on the corner!
Peyo
30

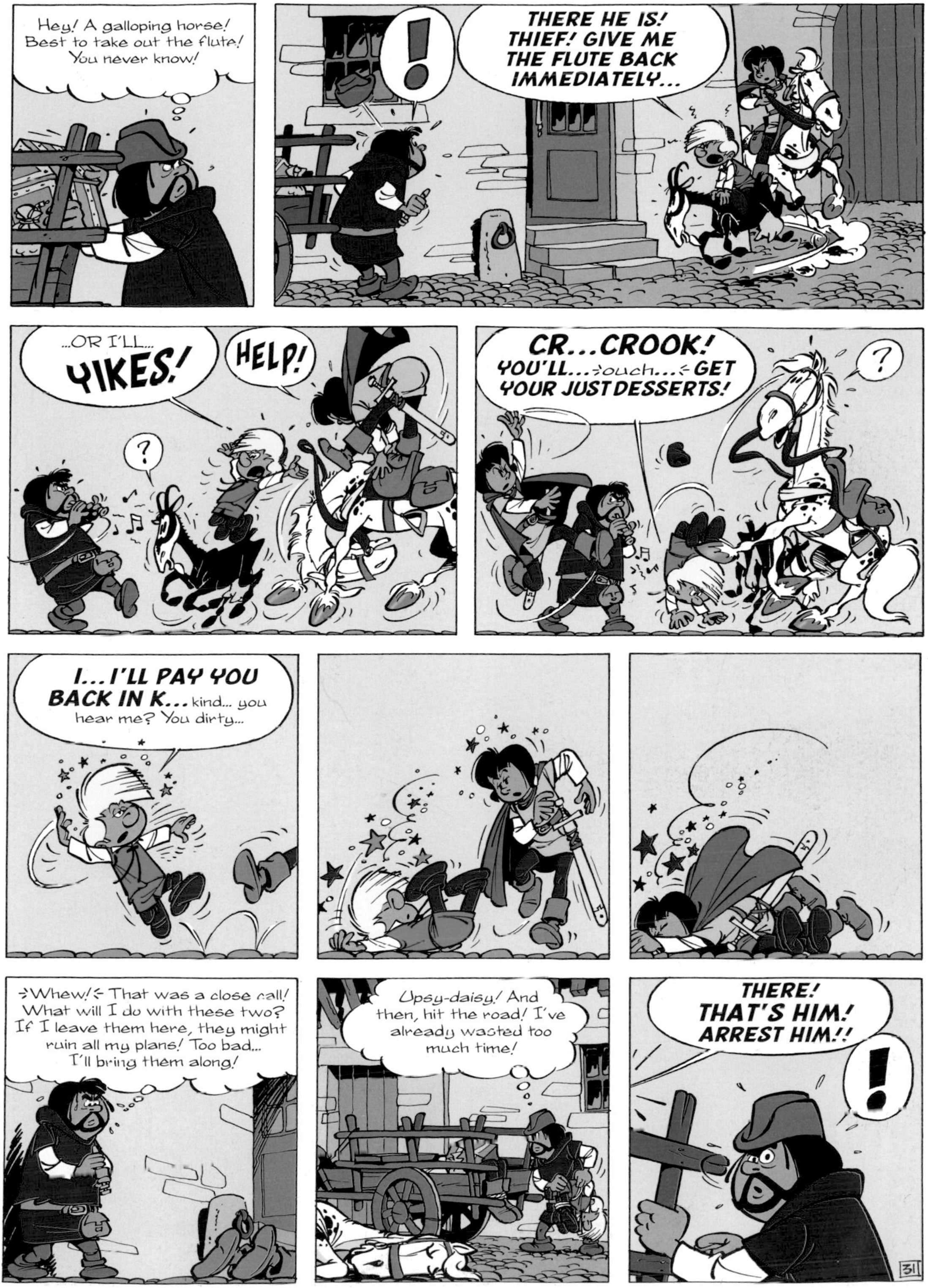
Hey! A galloping horse! Best to take out the flute! You never know!
!
THERE HE IS! THIEF! GIVE ME THE FLUTE BACK IMMEDIATELY...
...OR I'LL... YIKES!
HELP!
?
CR...CROOK! YOU'LL... ouch... GET YOUR JUST DESSERTS!
?
I... I'LL PAY YOU BACK IN K... kind... you hear me? You dirty...
Whew! That was a close call! What will I do with these two? If I leave them here, they might ruin all my plans! Too bad... I'll bring them along!
Upsy-daisy! And then, hit the road! I've already wasted too much time!
THERE! THAT'S HIM! ARREST HIM!!
!
31

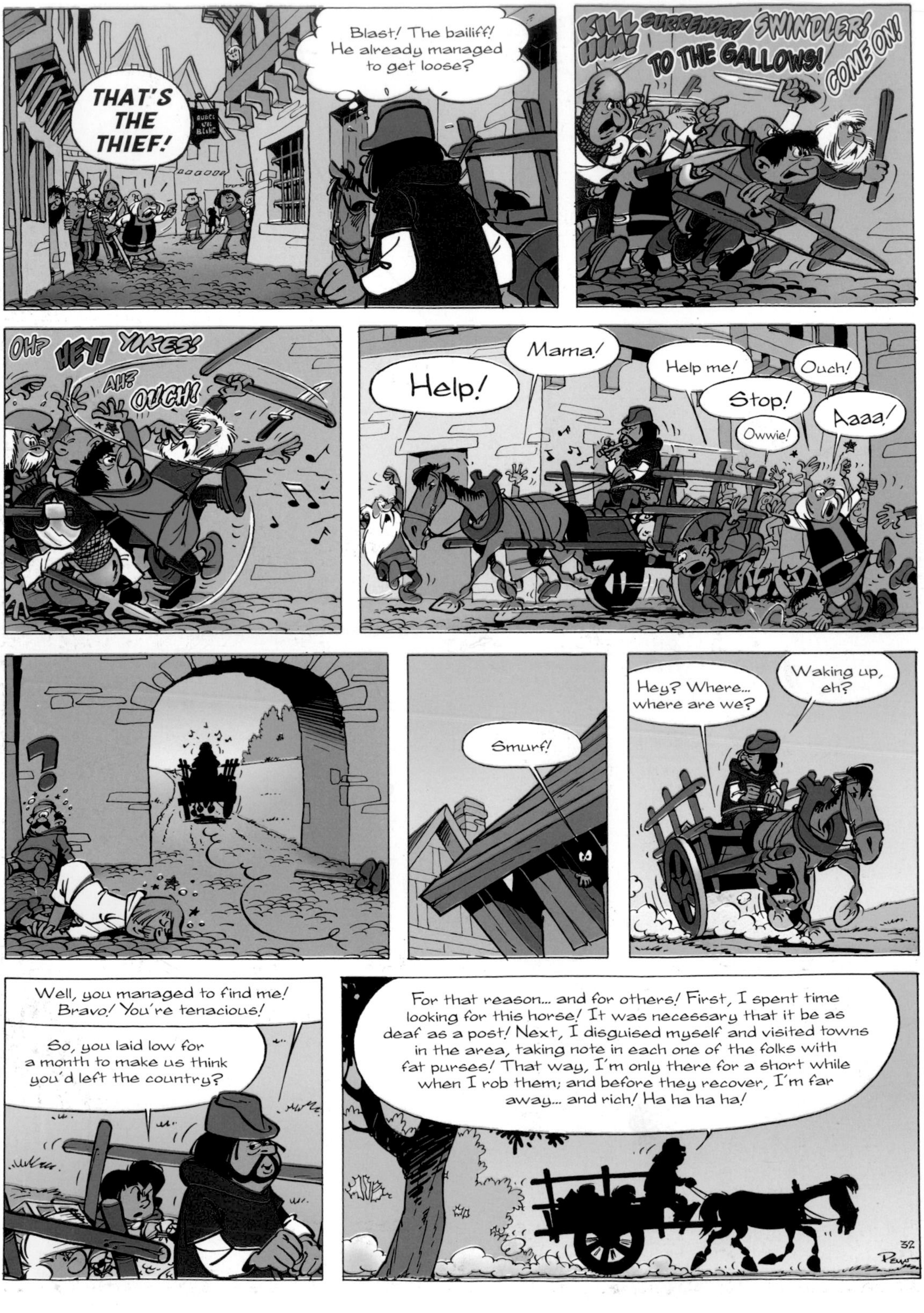
THAT'S THE THIEF!
Blast! The bailiff! He already managed to get loose?
KILL HIM!
SURRENDER!
SWINDLER!
TO THE GALLOWS!
COME ON!
OH?
HEY!
YIKES!
AH?
OUCH!
Help!
Mama!
Help me!
Ouch!
Stop!
Owwie!
Aaaa!
?
Smurf!
Hey? Where... where are we?
Waking up, eh?
Well, you managed to find me! Bravo! You're tenacious!
So, you laid low for a month to make us think you'd left the country?
For that reason... and for others! First, I spent time looking for this horse! It was necessary that it be as deaf as a post! Next, I disguised myself and visited towns in the area, taking note in each one of the folks with fat purses! That way, I'm only there for a short while when I rob them; and before they recover, I'm far away... and rich! Ha ha ha ha!

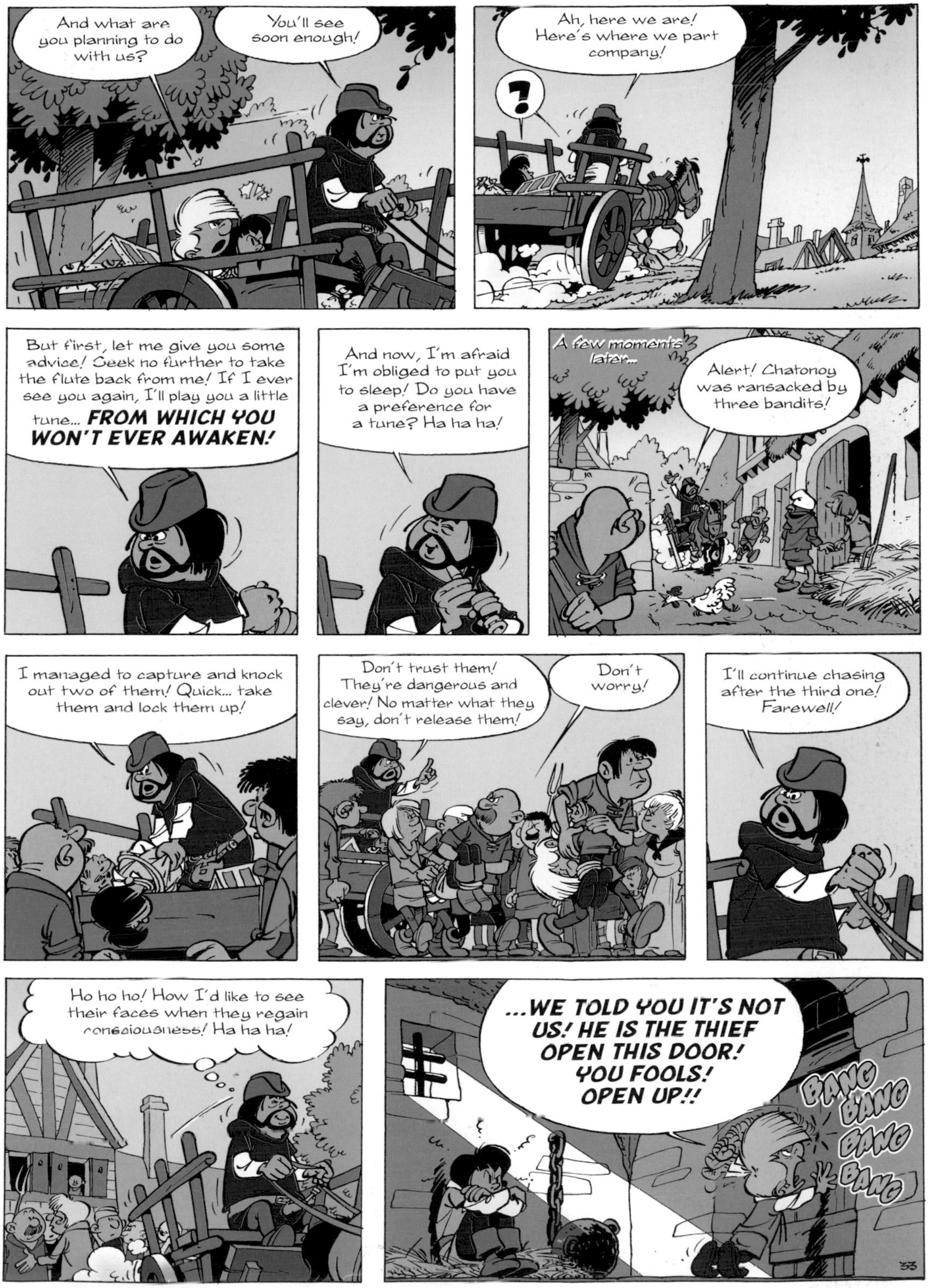
And what are you planning to do with us?
You'll see soon enough!
Ah, here we are! Here's where we part company!
?
But first, let me give you some advice! Seek no further to take the flute back from me! If I ever see you again, I'll play you a little tune... FROM WHICH YOU WON'T EVER AWAKEN!
And now, I'm afraid I'm obliged to put you to sleep! Do you have a preference for a tune? Ha ha ha!
A few moments later...
Alert! Chatonoy was ransacked by three bandits!
I managed to capture and knock out two of them! Quick... take them and lock them up!
Don't trust them! They're dangerous and clever! No matter what they say, don't release them!
Don't worry!
I'll continue chasing after the third one! Farewell!
Ho ho ho! How I'd like to see their faces when they regain consciousness! Ha ha ha!
...WE TOLD YOU IT'S NOT US! HE IS THE THIEF OPEN THIS DOOR! YOU FOOLS! OPEN UP!!
BANG BANG BANG BANG

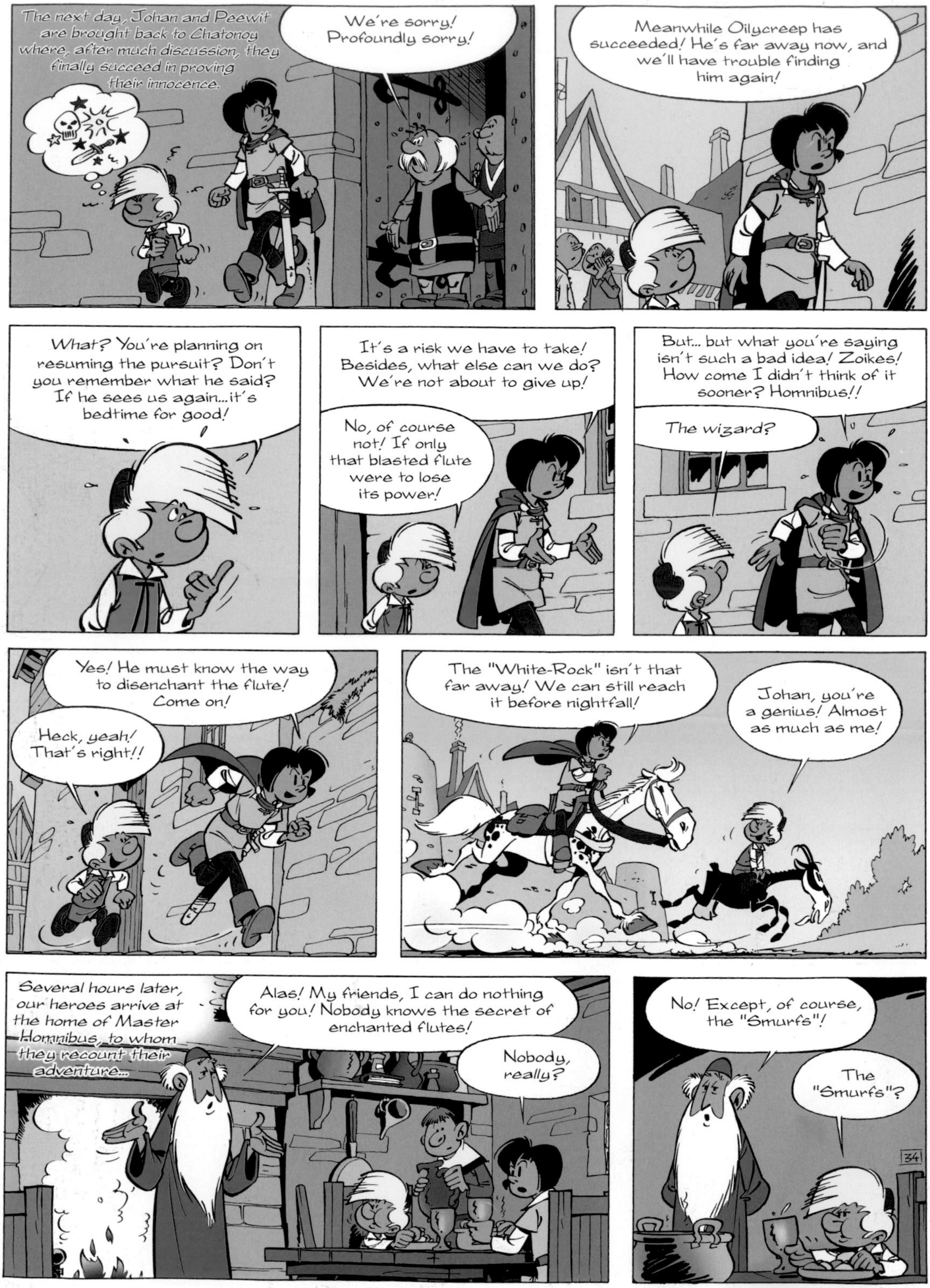
The next day, Johan and Peewit are brought back to Chatonoy where, after much discussion, they finally succeed in proving their innocence.
We're sorry! Profoundly sorry!
Meanwhile Oilycreep has succeeded! He's far away now, and we'll have trouble finding him again!
What? You're planning on resuming the pursuit? Don't you remember what he said? If he sees us again... it's bedtime for good!
It's a risk we have to take! Besides, what else can we do? We're not about to give up!
No, of course not! If only that blasted flute were to lose its power!
But... but what you're saying isn't such a bad idea! Zoikes! How come I didn't think of it sooner? Homnibus!!
The wizard?
Yes! He must know the way to disenchant the flute! Come on!
Heck, yeah! That's right!!
The "White-Rock" isn't that far away! We can still reach it before nightfall!
Johan, you're a genius! Almost as much as me!
Several hours later, our heroes arrive at the home of Master Homnibus, to whom they recount their adventure...
Alas! My friends, I can do nothing for you! Nobody knows the secret of enchanted flutes!
Nobody, really?
No! Except, of course, the "Smurfs"!
The "Smurfs"?
34

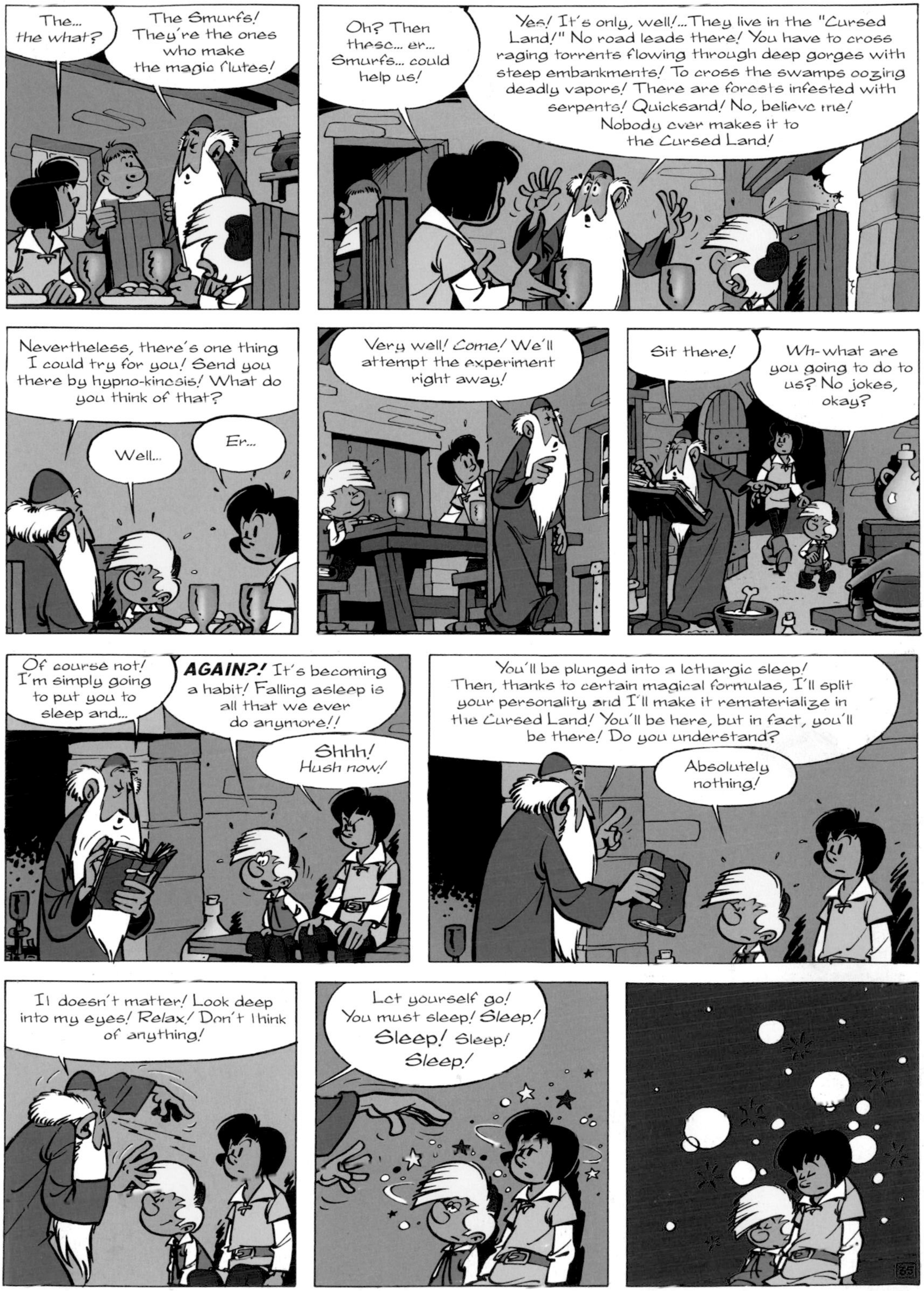
The... the what?
The Smurfs! They're the ones who make the magic flutes!
Oh? Then these... er... Smurfs... could help us!
Yes! It's only, well!...They live in the "Cursed Land!" No road leads there! You have to cross raging torrents flowing through deep gorges with steep embankments! To cross the swamps oozing deadly vapors! There are forests infested with serpents! Quicksand! No, believe me! Nobody ever makes it to the Cursed Land!
Nevertheless, there's one thing I could try for you! Send you there by hypno-kinesis! What do you think of that?
Well...
Er...
Very well! Come! We'll attempt the experiment right away!
Sit there!
Wh-what are you going to do to us? No jokes, okay?
Of course not! I'm simply going to put you to sleep and...
AGAIN?! It's becoming a habit! Falling asleep is all that we ever do anymore!!
Shhh! Hush now!
You'll be plunged into a lethargic sleep! Then, thanks to certain magical formulas, I'll split your personality and I'll make it rematerialize in the Cursed Land! You'll be here, but in fact, you'll be there! Do you understand?
Absolutely nothing!
It doesn't matter! Look deep into my eyes! Relax! Don't think of anything!
Let yourself go! You must sleep! Sleep! Sleep! Sleep! Sleep!
35

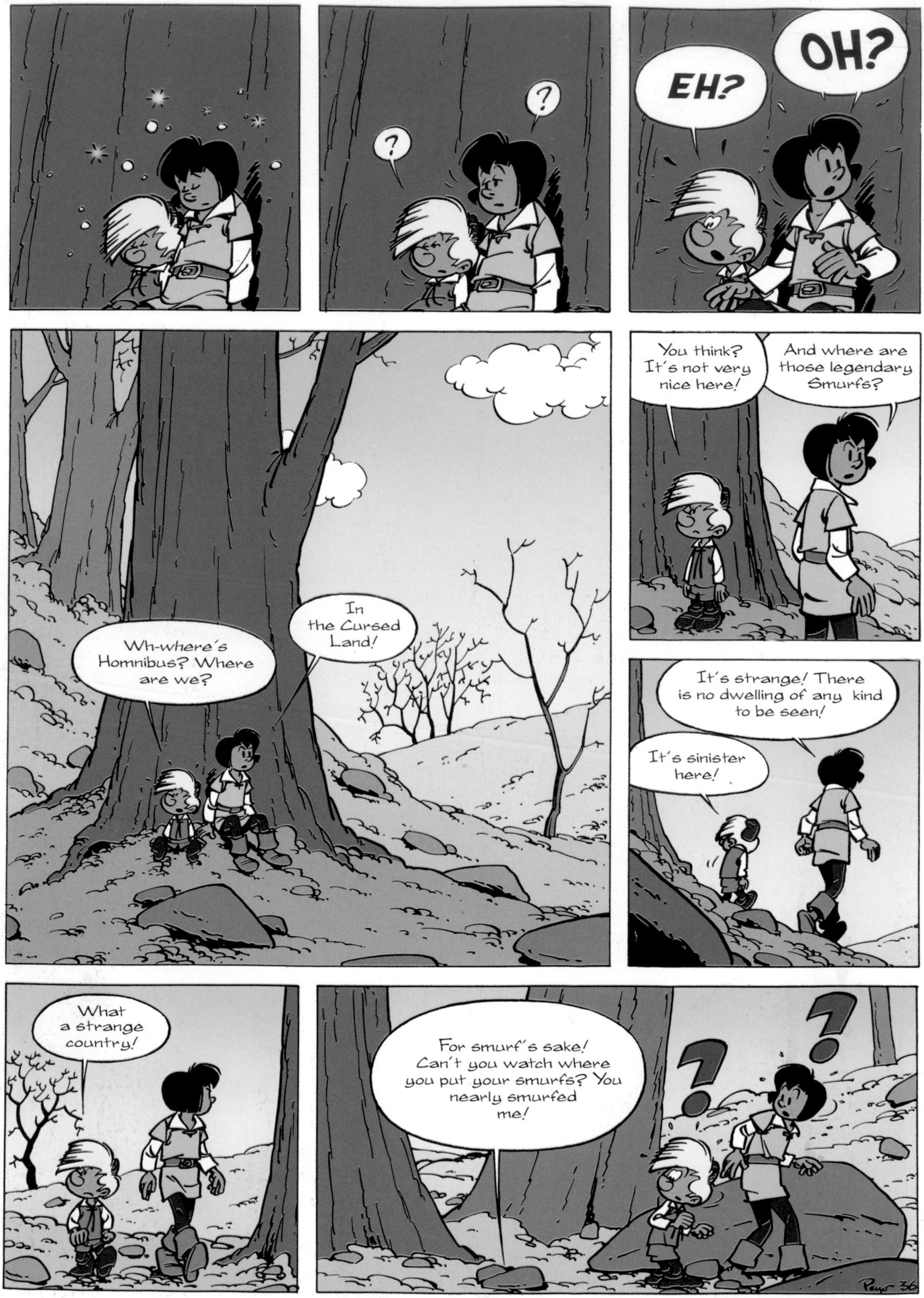
?
?
EH?
OH?
Wh-where's Homnibus? Where are we?
In the Cursed Land!
You think? It's not very nice here!
And where are those legendary Smurfs?
It's strange! There is no dwelling of any kind to be seen!
It's sinister here!
What a strange country!
For smurf's sake! Can't you watch where you put your smurfs? You nearly smurfed me!
Peyo 36

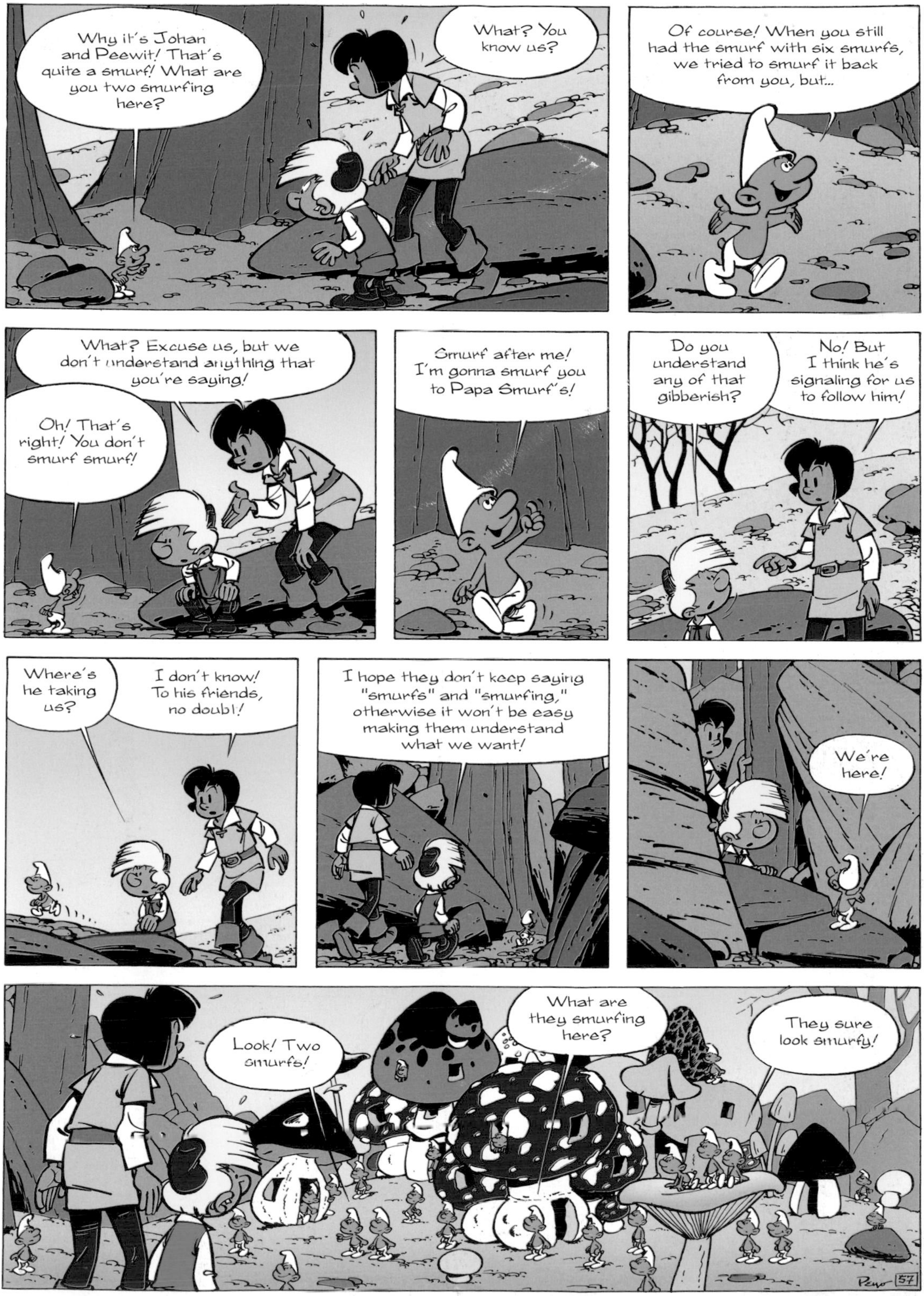
Why it's Johan and Peewit! That's quite a smurf! What are you two smurfing here?
What? You know us?
Of course! When you still had the smurf with six smurfs, we tried to smurf it back from you, but...
What? Excuse us, but we don't understand anything that you're saying!
Oh! That's right! You don't smurf smurf!
Smurf after me! I'm gonna smurf you to Papa Smurf's!
Do you understand any of that gibberish?
No! But I think he's signaling for us to follow him!
Where's he taking us?
I don't know! To his friends, no doubt!
I hope they don't keep saying "smurfs" and "smurfing," otherwise it won't be easy making them understand what we want!
We're here!
Look! Two smurfs!
What are they smurfing here?
They sure look smurfy!
Peyo 57

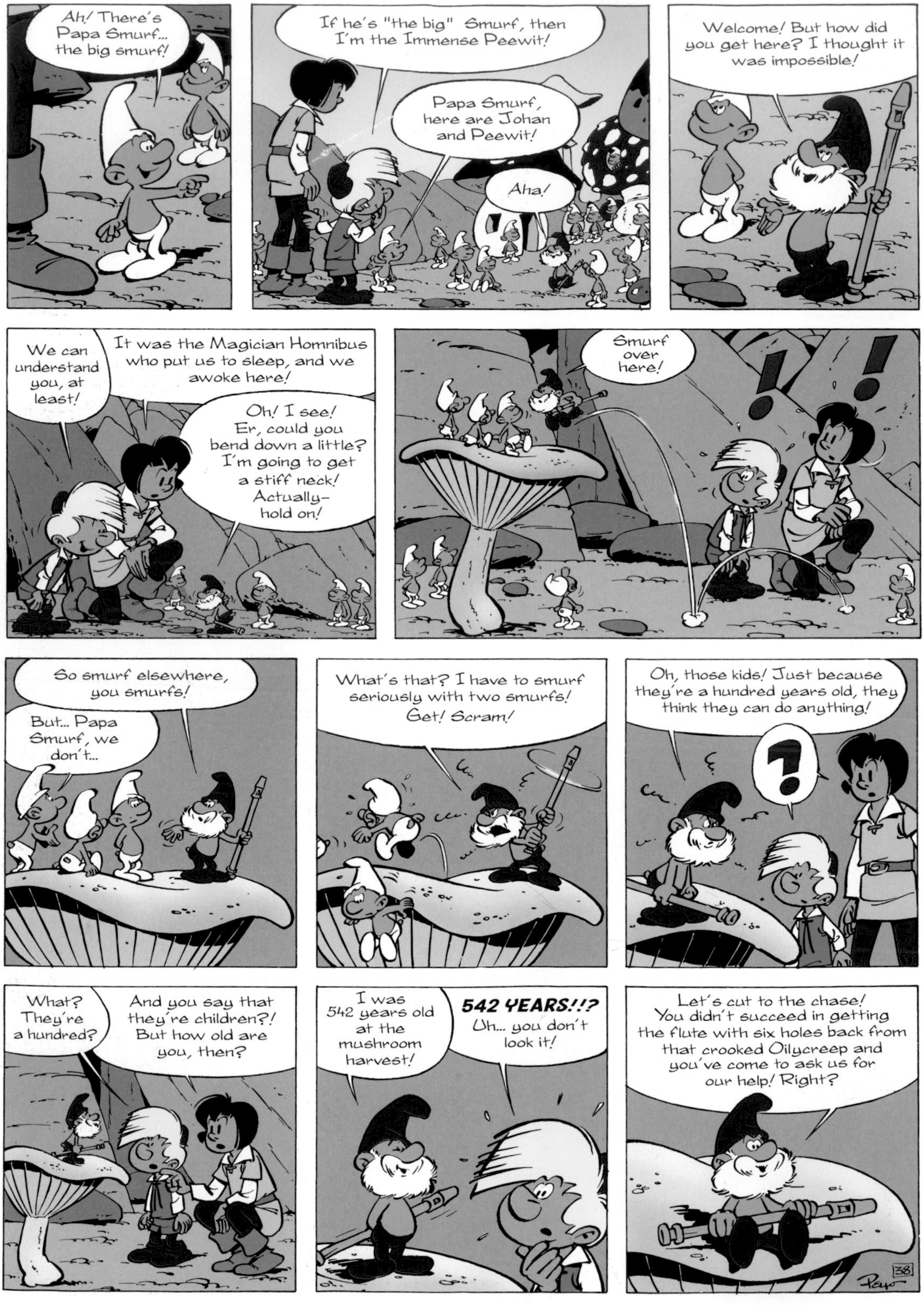

Ah! There's Papa Smurf... the big smurf!
If he's "the big" Smurf, then I'm the Immense Peewit!
Papa Smurf, here are Johan and Peewit!
Aha!
Welcome! But how did you get here? I thought it was impossible!
We can understand you, at least!
It was the Magician Homnibus who put us to sleep, and we awoke here!
Oh! I see! Er, could you bend down a little? I'm going to get a stiff neck! Actually- hold on!
Smurf over here!
So smurf elsewhere, you smurfs!
But... Papa Smurf, we don't...
What's that? I have to smurf seriously with two smurfs! Get! Scram!
Oh, those kids! Just because they're a hundred years old, they think they can do anything!
What? They're a hundred?
And you say that they're children?! But how old are you, then?
I was 542 years old at the mushroom harvest!
542 YEARS!!?
Uh... you don't look it!
Let's cut to the chase! You didn't succeed in getting the flute with six holes back from that crooked Oilycreep and you've come to ask us for our help! Right?
38
Peyo

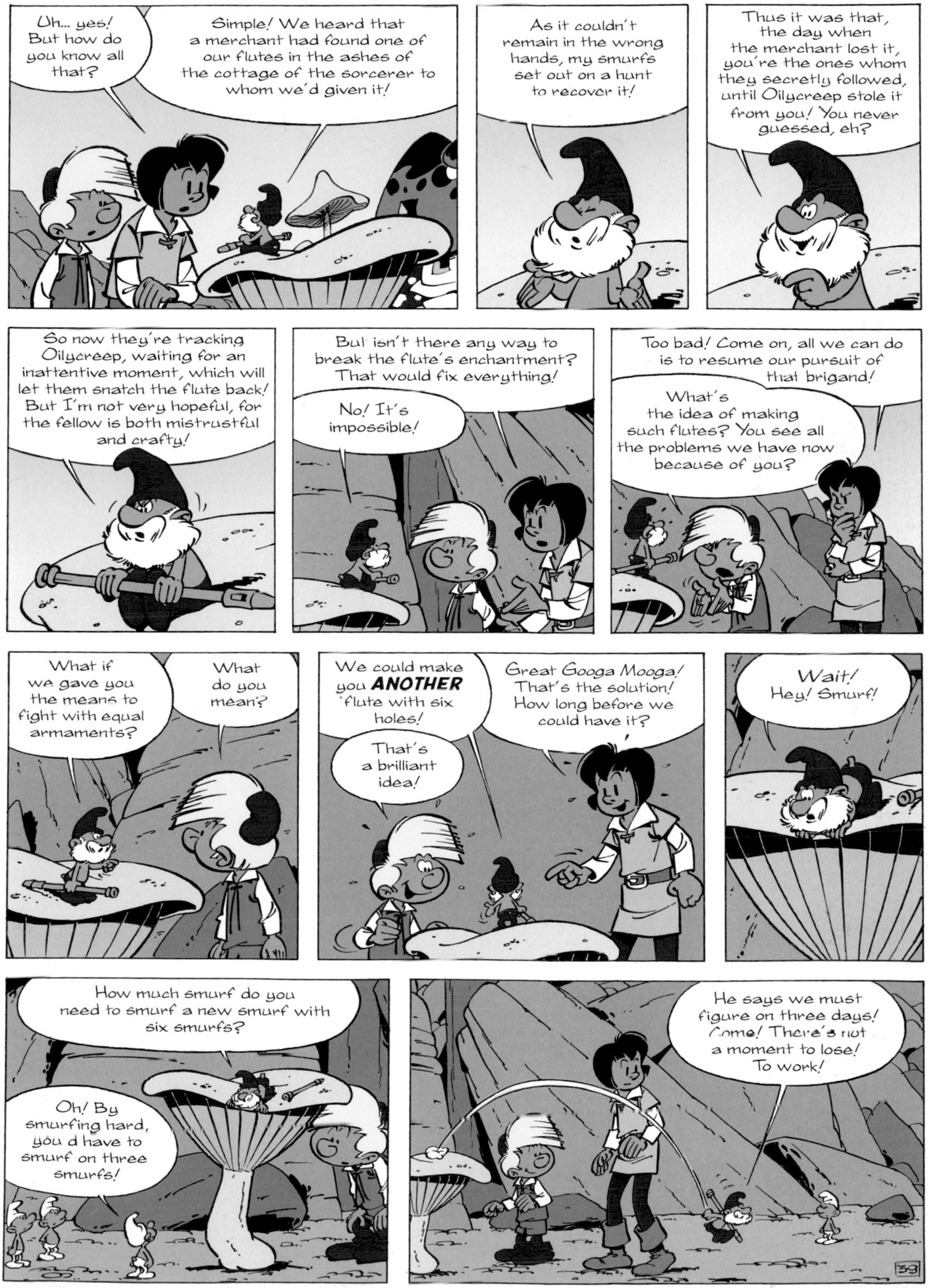
Uh... yes! But how do you know all that?
Simple! We heard that a merchant had found one of our flutes in the ashes of the cottage of the sorcerer to whom we'd given it!
As it couldn't remain in the wrong hands, my smurfs set out on a hunt to recover it!
Thus it was that, the day when the merchant lost it, you're the ones whom they secretly followed, until Oilycreep stole it from you! You never guessed, eh?
So now they're tracking Oilycreep, waiting for an inattentive moment, which will let them snatch the flute back! But I'm not very hopeful, for the fellow is both mistrustful and crafty!
But isn't there any way to break the flute's enchantment? That would fix everything!
No! It's impossible!
Too bad! Come on, all we can do is to resume our pursuit of that brigand!
What's the idea of making such flutes? You see all the problems we have now because of you?
What if we gave you the means to fight with equal armaments?
What do you mean?
We could make you ANOTHER flute with six holes!
Great Googa Mooga! That's the solution! How long before we could have it?
That's a brilliant idea!
Wait! Hey! Smurf!
How much smurf do you need to smurf a new smurf with six smurfs?
Oh! By smurfing hard, you'd have to smurf on three smurfs!
He says we must figure on three days! Come! There's not a moment to lose! To work!
39

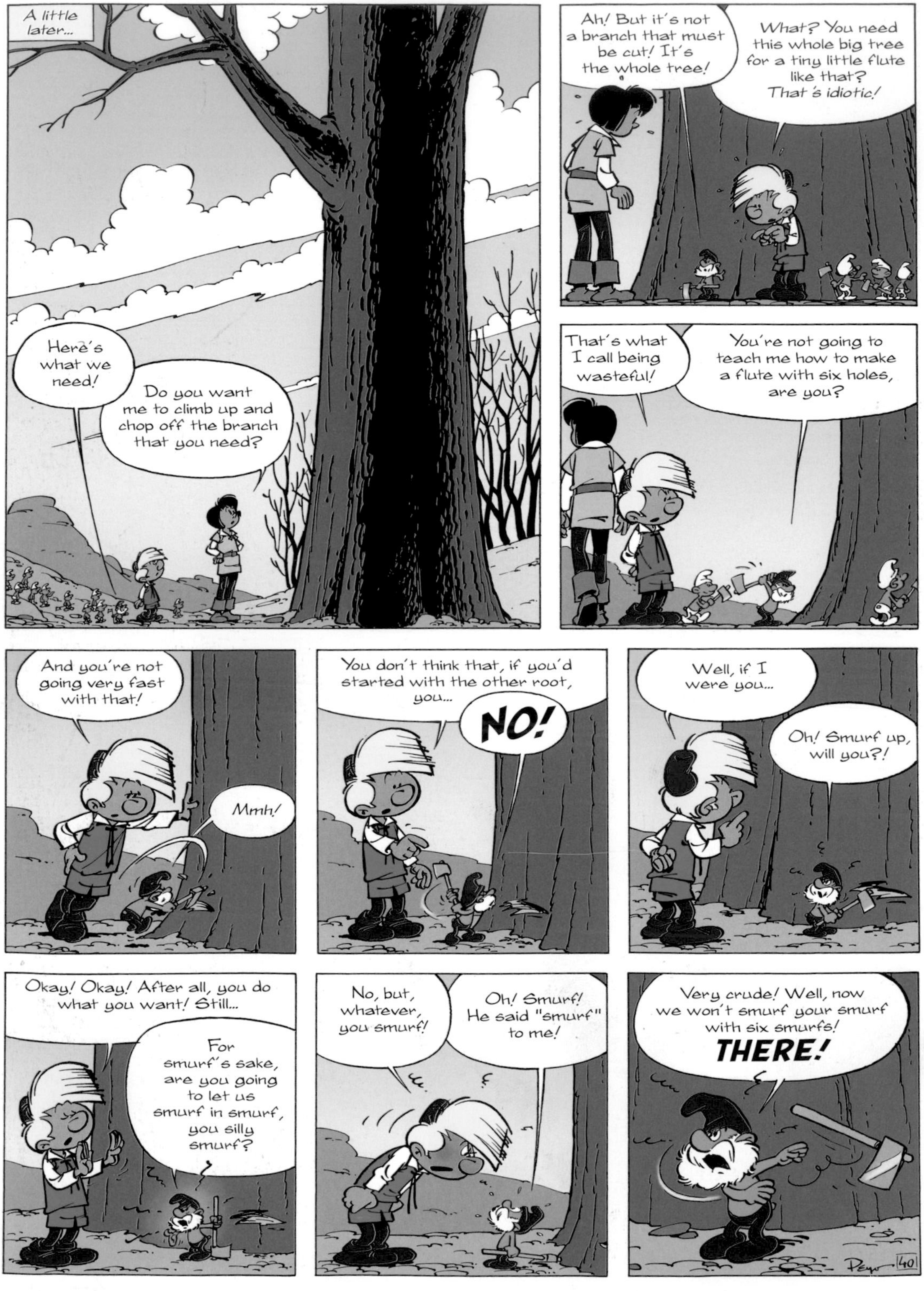
A little later...
Here's what we need!
Do you want me to climb up and chop off the branch that you need?
Ah! But it's not a branch that must be cut! It's the whole tree!
What? You need this whole big tree for a tiny little flute like that? That's idiotic!
That's what I call being wasteful!
You're not going to teach me how to make a flute with six holes, are you?
And you're not going very fast with that!
Mmh!
You don't think that, if you'd started with the other root, you...
NO!
Well, if I were you...
Oh! Smurf up, will you?!
Okay! Okay! After all, you do what you want! Still...
For smurf's sake, are you going to let us smurf in smurf, you silly smurf?
No, but, whatever, you smurf!
Oh! Smurf! He said "smurf" to me!
Very crude! Well, now we won't smurf your smurf with six smurfs!
THERE!
Peyo 40

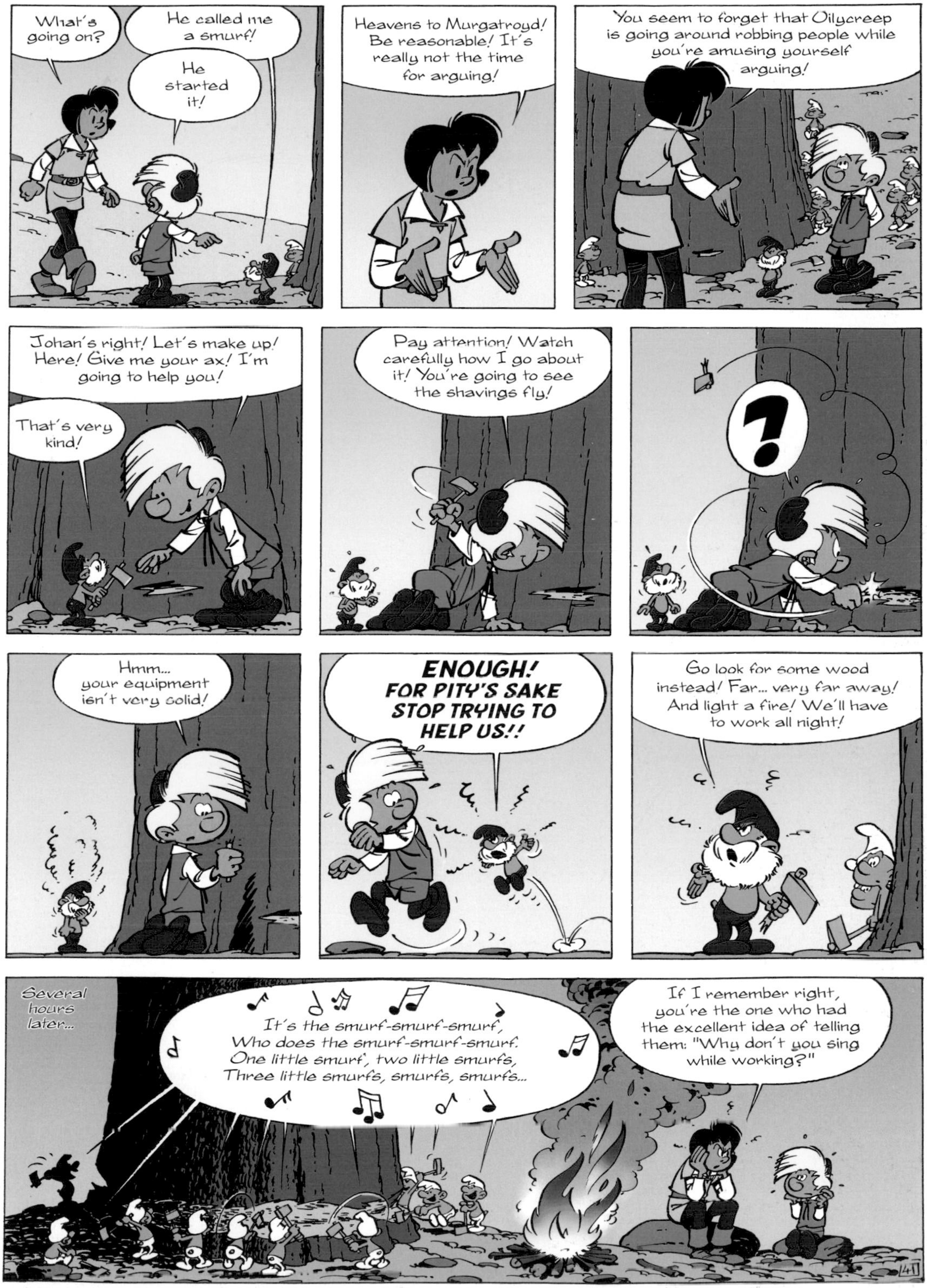
What's going on?
He called me a smurf!
He started it!
Heavens to Murgatroyd! Be reasonable! It's really not the time for arguing!
You seem to forget that Oilycreep is going around robbing people while you're amusing yourself arguing!
Johan's right! Let's make up! Here! Give me your ax! I'm going to help you!
That's very kind!
Pay attention! Watch carefully how I go about it! You're going to see the shavings fly!
?
Hmm... your equipment isn't very solid!
ENOUGH! FOR PITY'S SAKE STOP TRYING TO HELP US!!
Go look for some wood instead! Far... very far away! And light a fire! We'll have to work all night!
Several hours later...
It's the smurf-smurf-smurf, Who does the smurf-smurf-smurf. One little smurf, two little smurfs, Three little smurfs, smurfs, smurfs...
If I remember right, you're the one who had the excellent idea of telling them: "Why don't you sing while working?"
41

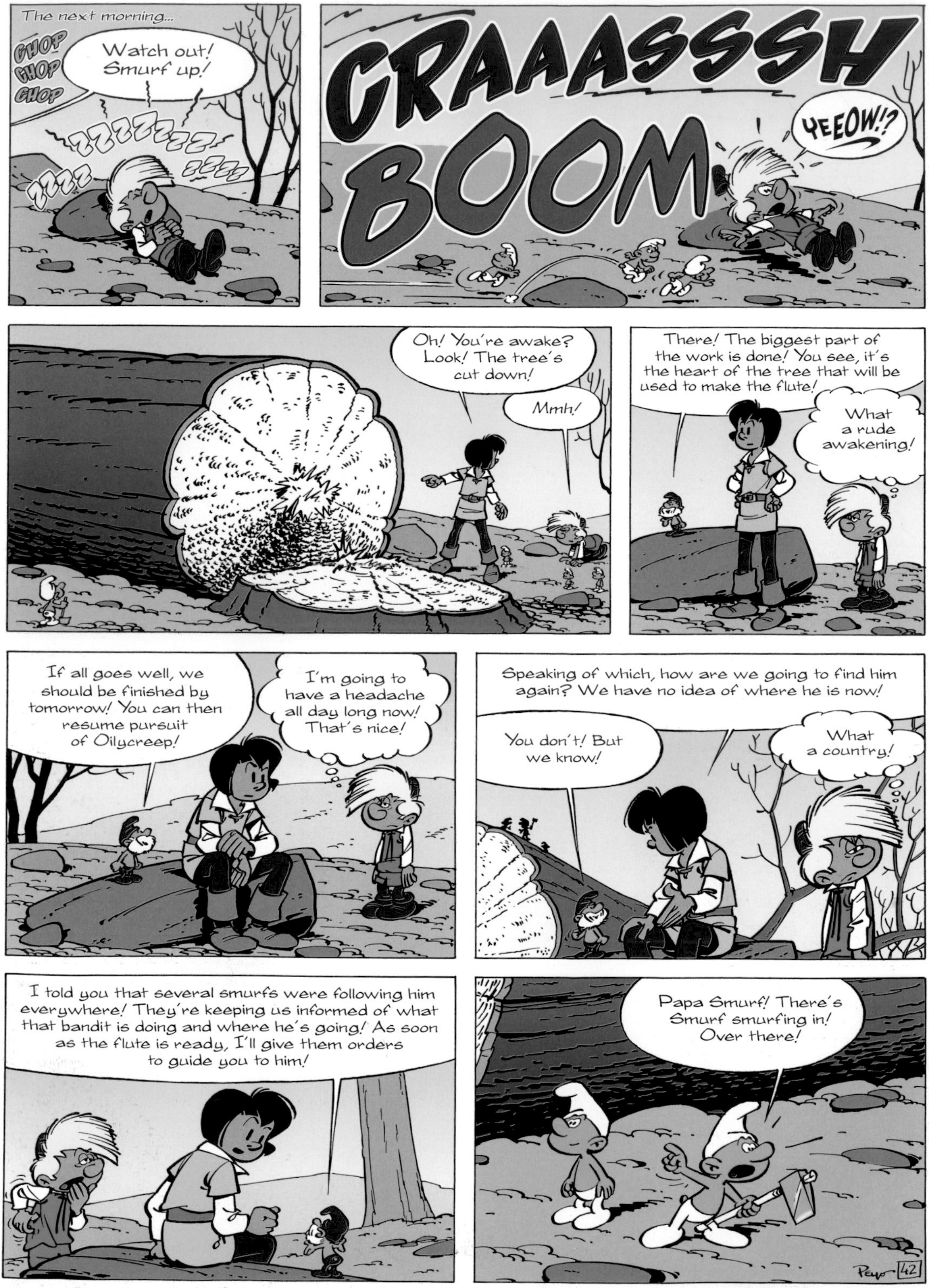
The next morning...
CHOP CHOP CHOP
Watch out! Smurf up!
ZZZZZZZZ
CRAAASSSH
BOOM
YEEOW!?
Oh! You're awake? Look! The tree's cut down!
Mmh!
There! The biggest part of the work is done! You see, it's the heart of the tree that will be used to make the flute!
What a rude awakening!
If all goes well, we should be finished by tomorrow! You can then resume pursuit of Oilycreep!
I'm going to have a headache all day long now! That's nice!
Speaking of which, how are we going to find him again? We have no idea of where he is now!
You don't! But we know!
What a country!
I told you that several smurfs were following him everywhere! They're keeping us informed of what that bandit is doing and where he's going! As soon as the flute is ready, I'll give them orders to guide you to him!
Papa Smurf! There's Smurf smurfing in! Over there!
Peyo 42

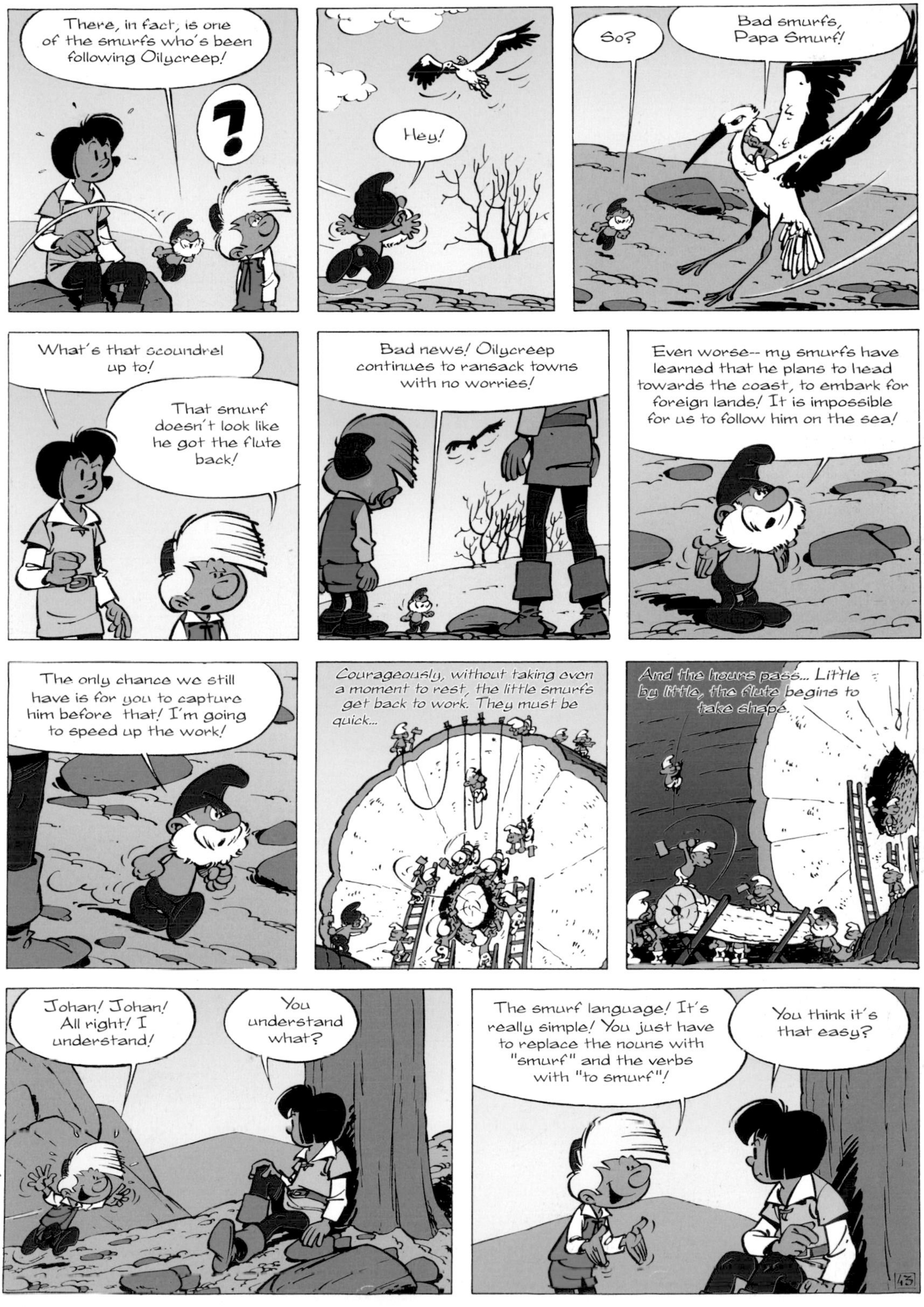

There, in fact, is one of the smurfs who's been following Oilycreep!
?
Hey!
So?
Bad smurfs, Papa Smurf!
What's that scoundrel up to!
That smurf doesn't look like he got the flute back!
Bad news! Oilycreep continues to ransack towns with no worries!
Even worse-- my smurfs have learned that he plans to head towards the coast, to embark for foreign lands! It is impossible for us to follow him on the sea!
The only chance we still have is for you to capture him before that! I'm going to speed up the work!
Courageously, without taking even a moment to rest, the little smurfs get back to work. They must be quick...
And the hours pass... Little by little, the flute begins to take shape.
Johan! Johan! All right! I understand!
You understand what?
The smurf language! It's really simple! You just have to replace the nouns with "smurf" and the verbs with "to smurf"!
You think it's that easy?
43

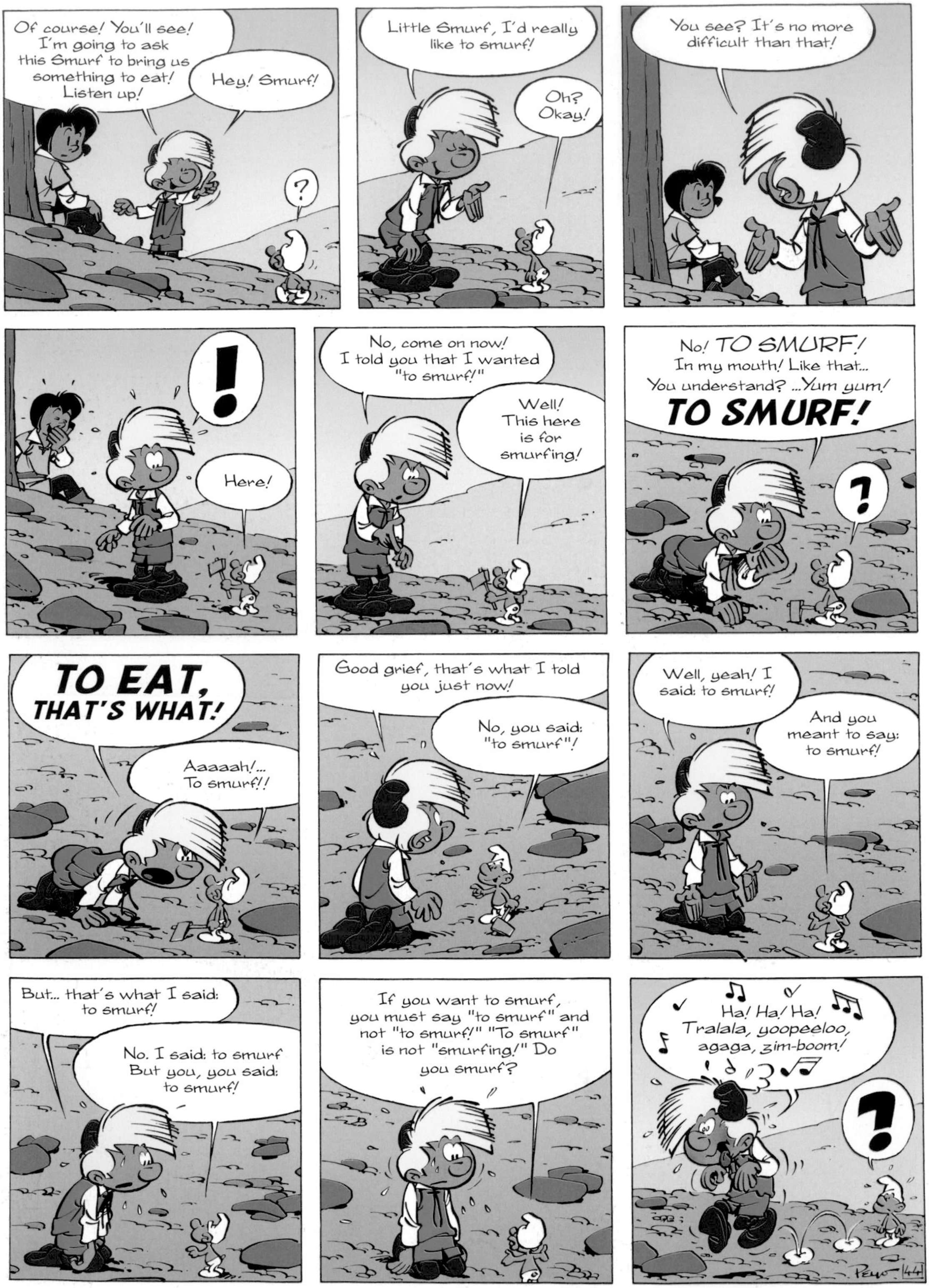
Of course! You'll see! I'm going to ask this Smurf to bring us something to eat! Listen up!
Hey! Smurf!
?
Little Smurf, I'd really like to smurf!
Oh? Okay!
You see? It's no more difficult than that!
!
Here!
No, come on now! I told you that I wanted "to smurf!"
Well! This here is for smurfing!
No! TO SMURF! In my mouth! Like that... You understand? ...Yum yum! TO SMURF!
?
TO EAT, THAT'S WHAT!
Aaaaah!... To smurf!!
Good grief, that's what I told you just now!
No, you said: "to smurf"!
Well, yeah! I said: to smurf!
And you meant to say: to smurf!
But... that's what I said: to smurf!
No. I said: to smurf But you, you said: to smurf!
If you want to smurf, you must say "to smurf" and not "to smurf!" "To smurf" is not "smurfing!" Do you smurf?
Ha! Ha! Ha! Tralala, yoopeeloo, agaga, zim-boom!
?

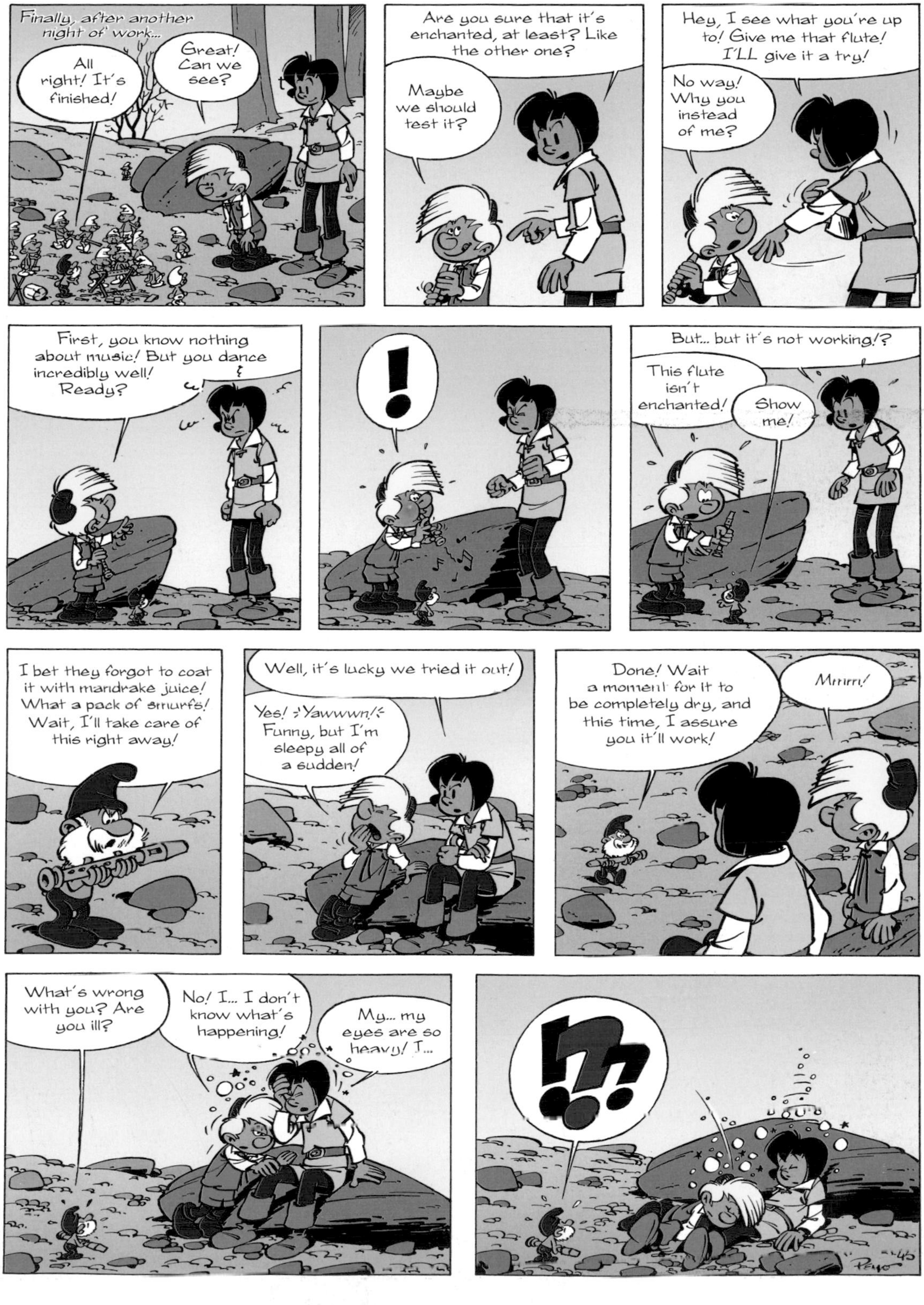
Finally, after another night of work...
All right! It's finished!
Great! Can we see?
Are you sure that it's enchanted, at least? Like the other one?
Maybe we should test it?
Hey, I see what you're up to! Give me that flute! I'LL give it a try!
No way! Why you instead of me?
First, you know nothing about music! But you dance incredibly well! Ready?
!
But... but it's not working!?
This flute isn't enchanted!
Show me!
I bet they forgot to coat it with mandrake juice! What a pack of smurfs! Wait, I'll take care of this right away!
Well, it's lucky we tried it out!
Yes! -Yawwwn!- Funny, but I'm sleepy all of a sudden!
Done! Wait a moment for it to be completely dry, and this time, I assure you it'll work!
Mrrrrr!
What's wrong with you? Are you ill?
No! I... I don't know what's happening!
My... my eyes are so heavy! I...
!??

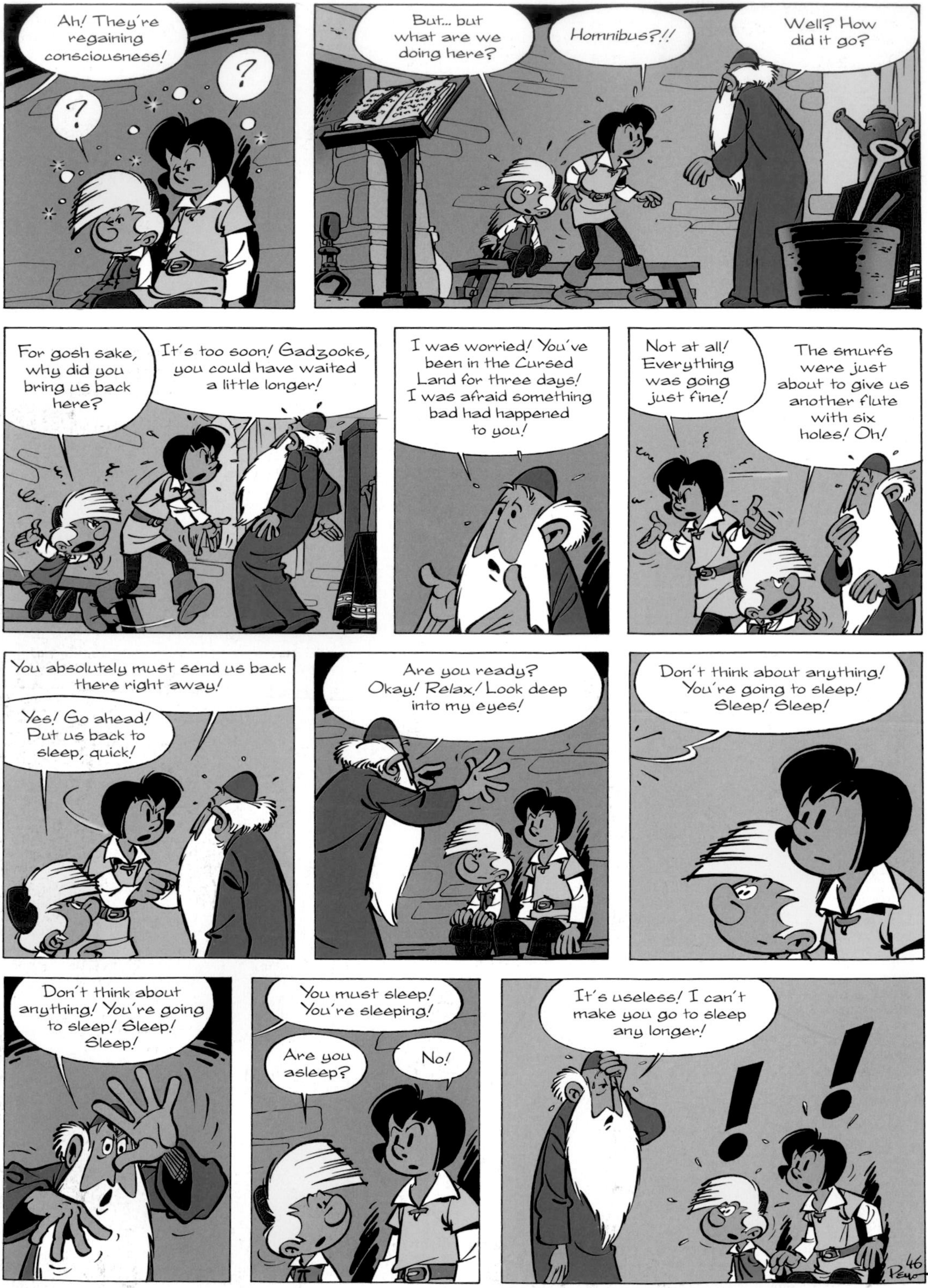
Ah! They're regaining consciousness!
?
?
But... but what are we doing here?
Homnibus?!!
Well? How did it go?
For gosh sake, why did you bring us back here?
It's too soon! Gadzooks, you could have waited a little longer!
I was worried! You've been in the Cursed Land for three days! I was afraid something bad had happened to you!
Not at all! Everything was going just fine!
The smurfs were just about to give us another flute with six holes! Oh!
You absolutely must send us back there right away!
Yes! Go ahead! Put us back to sleep, quick!
Are you ready? Okay! Relax! Look deep into my eyes!
Don't think about anything! You're going to sleep! Sleep! Sleep!
Don't think about anything! You're going to sleep! Sleep! Sleep!
You must sleep! You're sleeping!
Are you asleep?
No!
It's useless! I can't make you go to sleep any longer!
!!

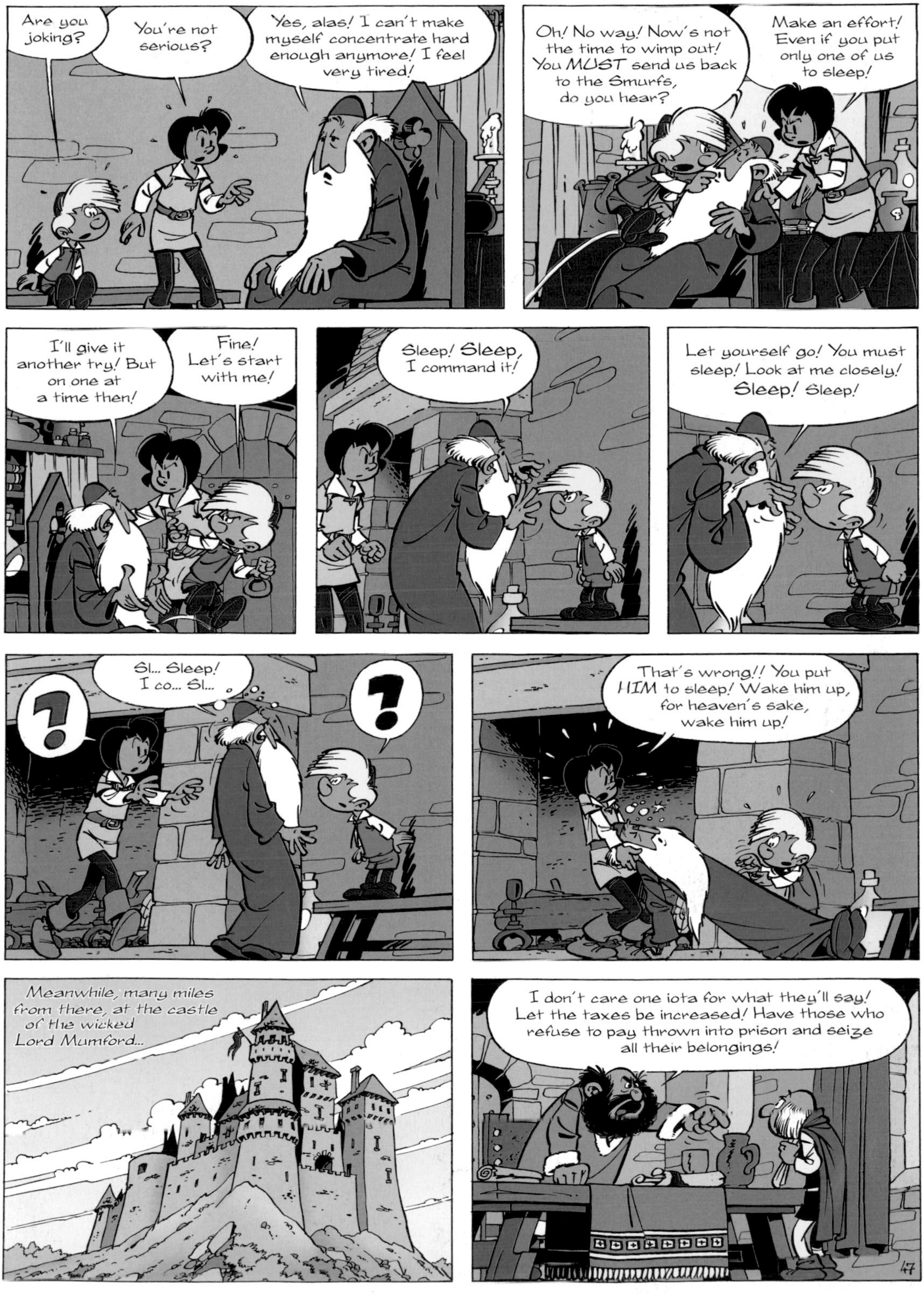
Are you joking?
You're not serious?
Yes, alas! I can't make myself concentrate hard enough anymore! I feel very tired!
Oh! No way! Now's not the time to wimp out! You MUST send us back to the Smurfs, do you hear?
Make an effort! Even if you put only one of us to sleep!
I'll give it another try! But on one at a time then!
Fine! Let's start with me!
Sleep! Sleep, I command it!
Let yourself go! You must sleep! Look at me closely! Sleep! Sleep!
?
Sl... Sleep! I co... Sl...
?
That's wrong!! You put HIM to sleep! Wake him up, for heaven's sake, wake him up!
Meanwhile, many miles from there, at the castle of the wicked Lord Mumford...
I don't care one iota for what they'll say! Let the taxes be increased! Have those who refuse to pay thrown into prison and seize all their belongings!
47

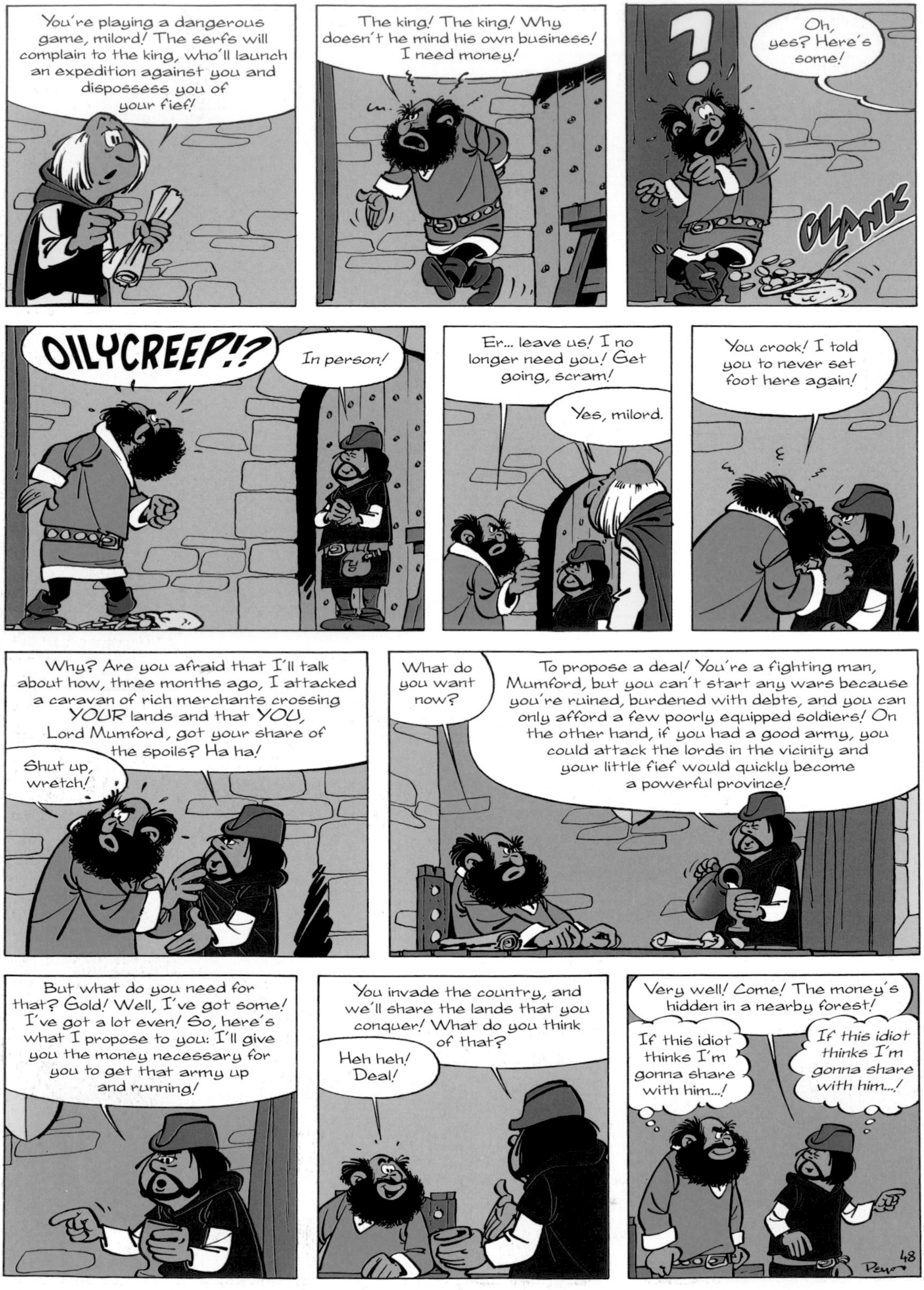
You're playing a dangerous game, milord! The serfs will complain to the king, who'll launch an expedition against you and dispossess you of your fief!
The king! The king! Why doesn't he mind his own business! I need money!
Oh, yes? Here's some!
CLANK
OILYCREEP!?
In person!
Er... leave us! I no longer need you! Get going, scram!
Yes, milord.
You crook! I told you to never set foot here again!
Why? Are you afraid that I'll talk about how, three months ago, I attacked a caravan of rich merchants crossing YOUR lands and that YOU, Lord Mumford, got your share of the spoils? Ha ha!
Shut up, wretch!
What do you want now?
To propose a deal! You're a fighting man, Mumford, but you can't start any wars because you're ruined, burdened with debts, and you can only afford a few poorly equipped soldiers! On the other hand, if you had a good army, you could attack the lords in the vicinity and your little fief would quickly become a powerful province!
But what do you need for that? Gold! Well, I've got some! I've got a lot even! So, here's what I propose to you: I'll give you the money necessary for you to get that army up and running!
You invade the country, and we'll share the lands that you conquer! What do you think of that?
Heh heh! Deal!
Very well! Come! The money's hidden in a nearby forest!
If this idiot thinks I'm gonna share with him...!
If this idiot thinks I'm gonna share with him...!
48
Peyo

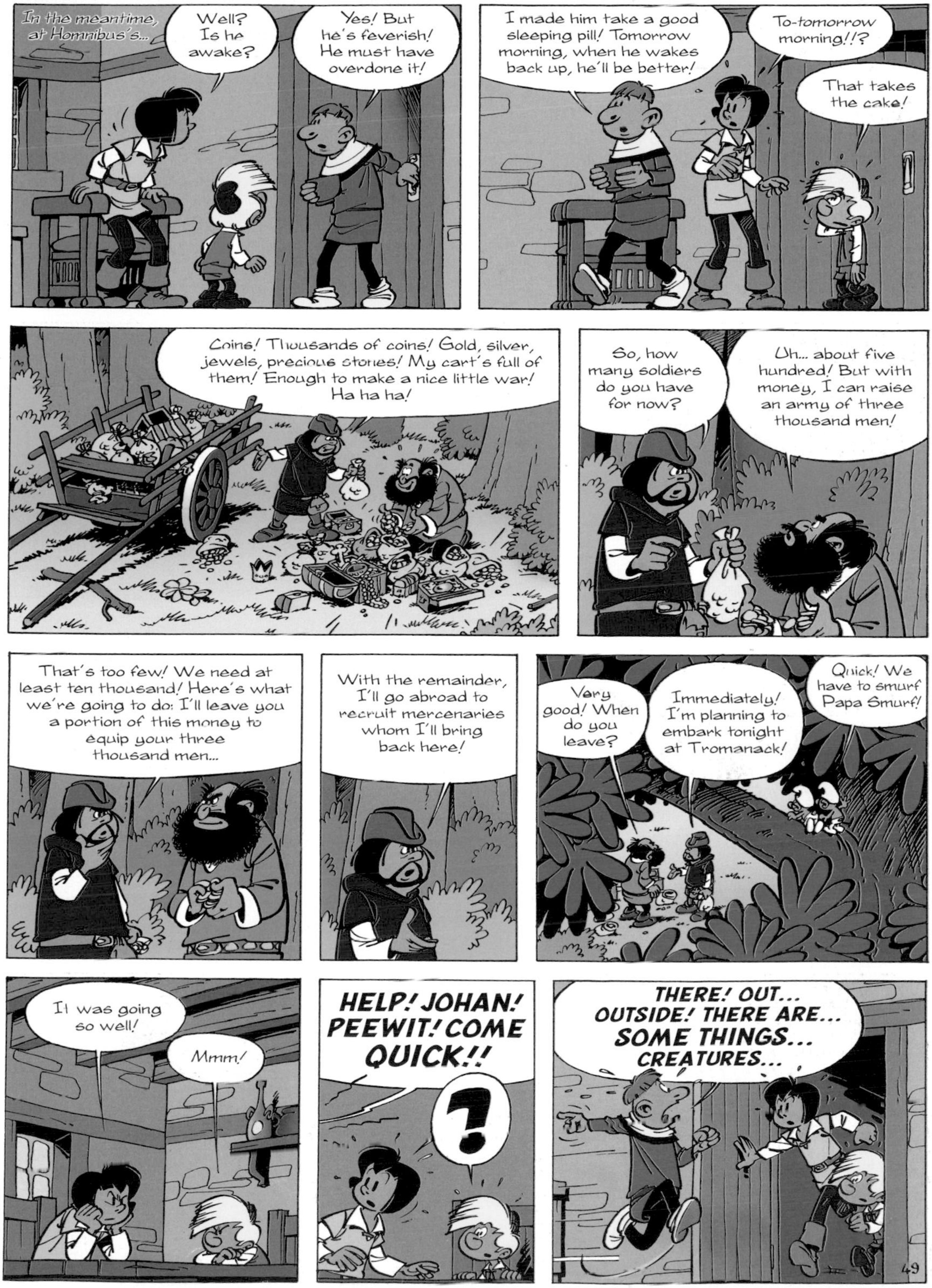

In the meantime, at Homnibus's...
Well? Is he awake?
Yes! But he's feverish! He must have overdone it!
I made him take a good sleeping pill! Tomorrow morning, when he wakes back up, he'll be better!
To-tomorrow morning!!?
That takes the cake!
Coins! Thousands of coins! Gold, silver, jewels, precious stones! My cart's full of them! Enough to make a nice little war! Ha ha ha!
So, how many soldiers do you have for now?
Uh... about five hundred! But with money, I can raise an army of three thousand men!
That's too few! We need at least ten thousand! Here's what we're going to do: I'll leave you a portion of this money to equip your three thousand men...
With the remainder, I'll go abroad to recruit mercenaries whom I'll bring back here!
Very good! When do you leave?
Immediately! I'm planning to embark tonight at Tromanack!
Quick! We have to smurf Papa Smurf!
It was going so well!
Mmm!
HELP! JOHAN! PEEWIT! COME QUICK!!
?
THERE! OUT... OUTSIDE! THERE ARE... SOME THINGS... CREATURES...
49

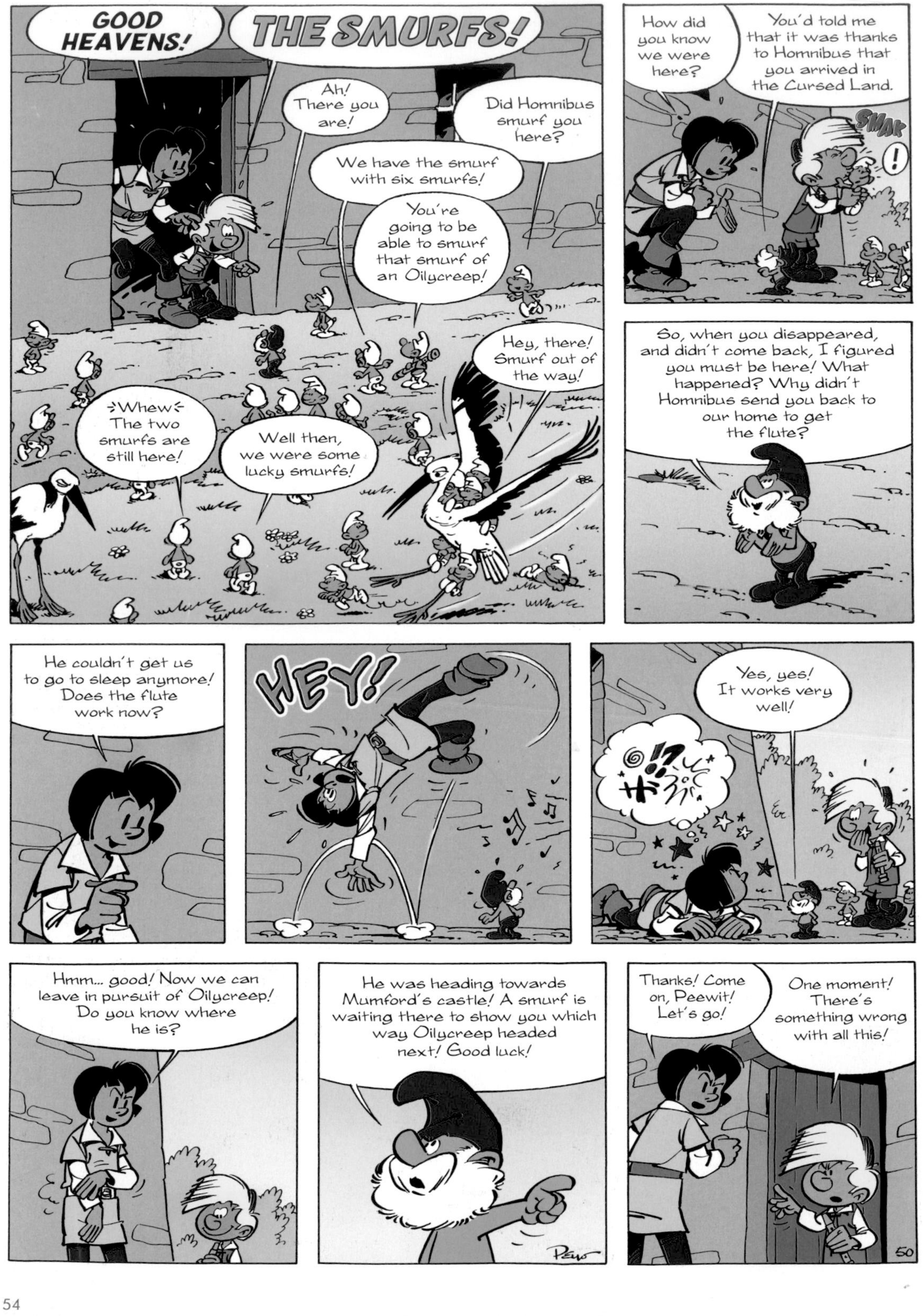
GOOD HEAVENS!
THE SMURFS!
Ah! There you are!
Did Homnibus smurf you here?
We have the smurf with six smurfs!
You're going to be able to smurf that smurf of an Oilycreep!
Hey, there! Smurf out of the way!
Whew The two smurfs are still here!
Well then, we were some lucky smurfs!
How did you know we were here?
You'd told me that it was thanks to Homnibus that you arrived in the Cursed Land.
SMAK
!
So, when you disappeared, and didn't come back, I figured you must be here! What happened? Why didn't Homnibus send you back to our home to get the flute?
He couldn't get us to go to sleep anymore! Does the flute work now?
HEY!
Yes, yes! It works very well!
Hmm... good! Now we can leave in pursuit of Oilycreep! Do you know where he is?
He was heading towards Mumford's castle! A smurf is waiting there to show you which way Oilycreep headed next! Good luck!
Thanks! Come on, Peewit! Let's go!
One moment! There's something wrong with all this!
50

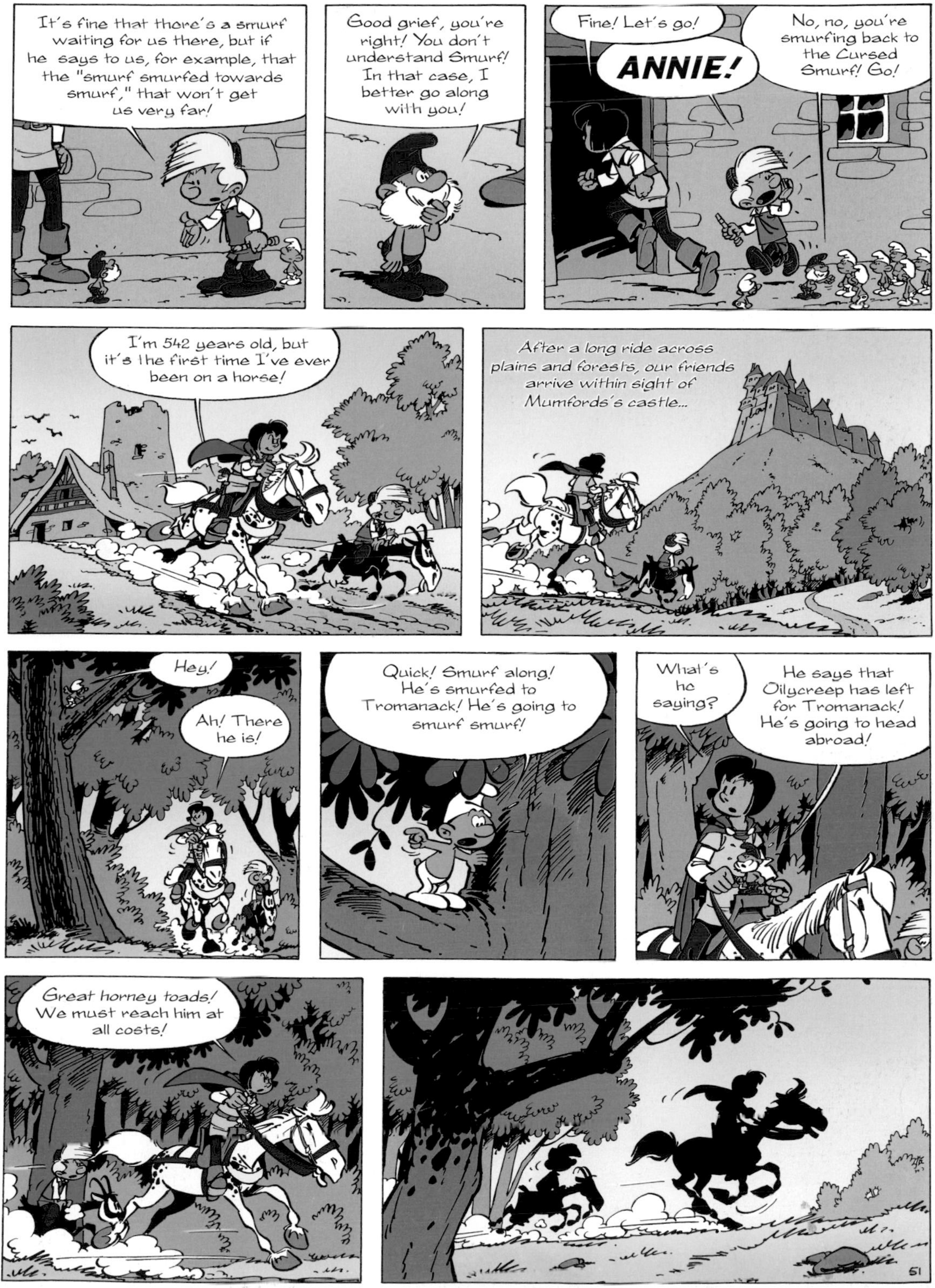
It's fine that there's a smurf waiting for us there, but if he says to us, for example, that the "smurf smurfed towards smurf," that won't get us very far!
Good grief, you're right! You don't understand Smurf! In that case, I better go along with you!
Fine! Let's go!
ANNIE!
No, no, you're smurfing back to the Cursed Smurf! Go!
I'm 542 years old, but it's the first time I've ever been on a horse!
After a long ride across plains and forests, our friends arrive within sight of Mumfords's castle...
Hey!
Ah! There he is!
Quick! Smurf along! He's smurfed to Tromanack! He's going to smurf smurf!
What's he saying?
He says that Oilycreep has left for Tromanack! He's going to head abroad!
Great horney toads! We must reach him at all costs!
51

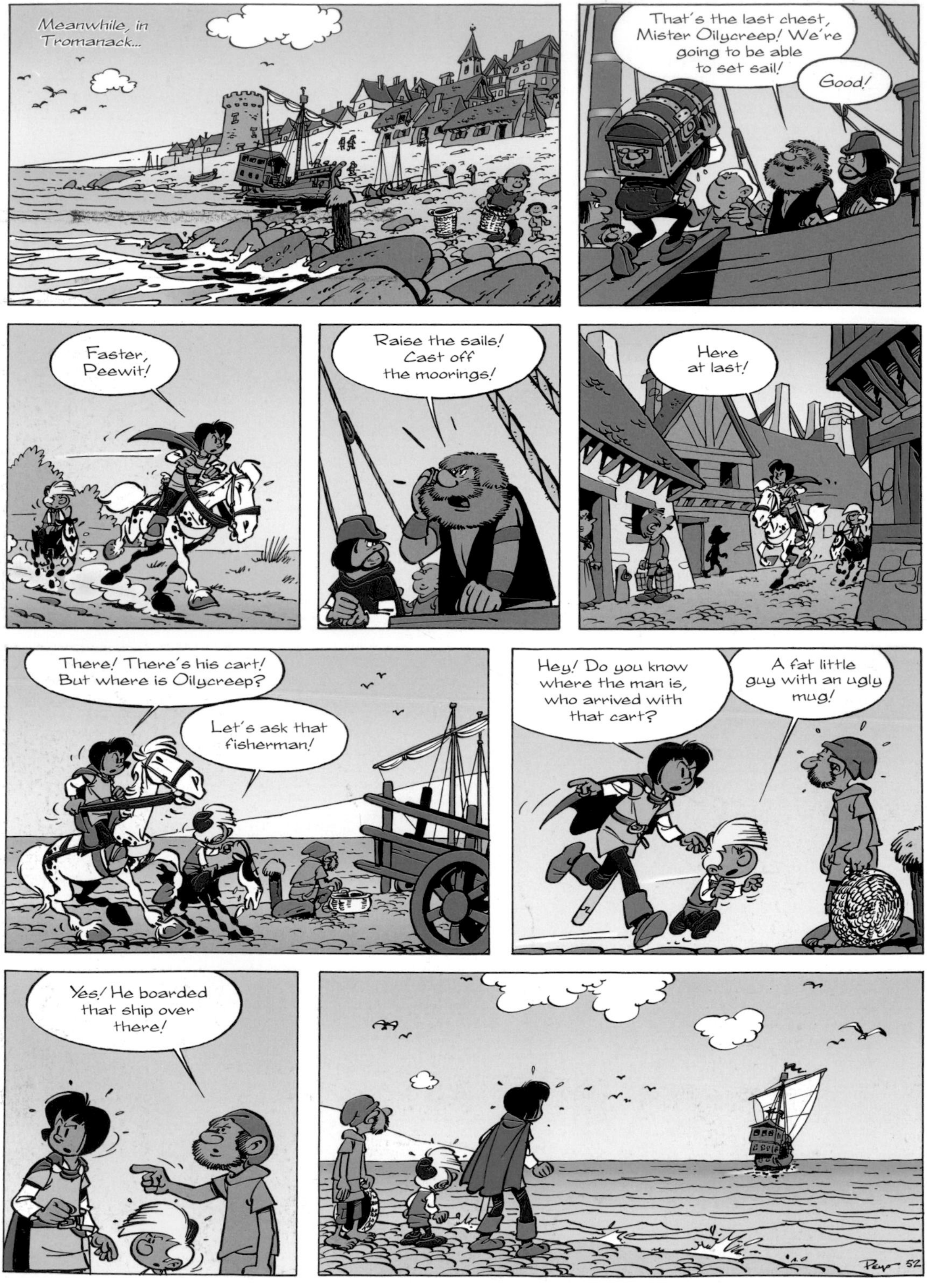

Meanwhile, in Tromanack...
That's the last chest, Mister Oilycreep! We're going to be able to set sail!
Good!
Faster, Peewit!
Raise the sails! Cast off the moorings!
Here at last!
There! There's his cart! But where is Oilycreep?
Let's ask that fisherman!
Hey! Do you know where the man is, who arrived with that cart?
A fat little guy with an ugly mug!
Yes! He boarded that ship over there!
Peyo 52

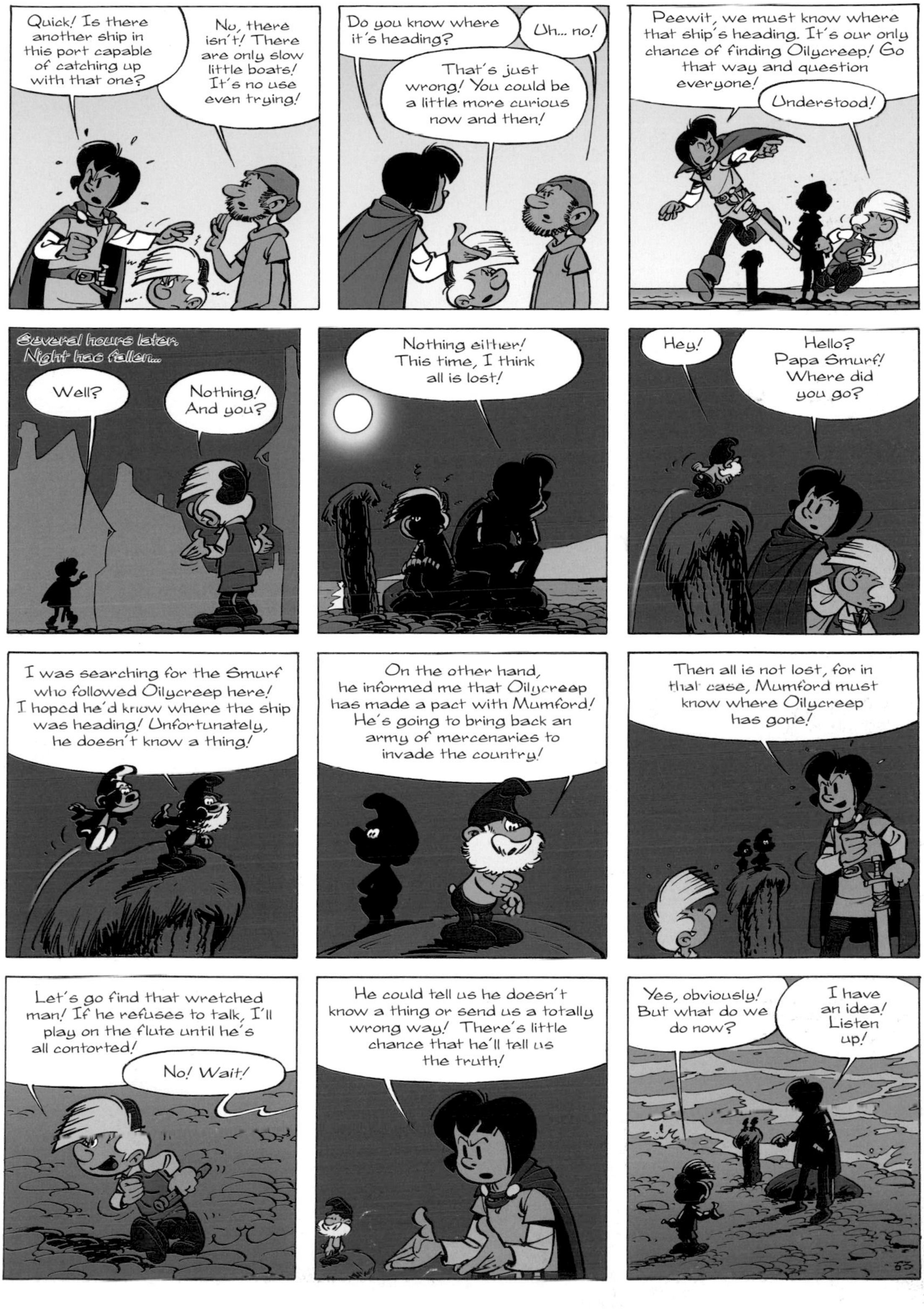

Quick! Is there another ship in this port capable of catching up with that one?
No, there isn't! There are only slow little boats! It's no use even trying!
Do you know where it's heading?
Uh... no!
That's just wrong! You could be a little more curious now and then!
Peewit, we must know where that ship's heading. It's our only chance of finding Oilycreep! Go that way and question everyone!
Understood!
Several hours later. Night has fallen...
Well?
Nothing! And you?
Nothing either! This time, I think all is lost!
Hey!
Hello? Papa Smurf! Where did you go?
I was searching for the Smurf who followed Oilycreep here! I hoped he'd know where the ship was heading! Unfortunately, he doesn't know a thing!
On the other hand, he informed me that Oilycreep has made a pact with Mumford! He's going to bring back an army of mercenaries to invade the country!
Then all is not lost, for in that case, Mumford must know where Oilycreep has gone!
Let's go find that wretched man! If he refuses to talk, I'll play on the flute until he's all contorted!
No! Wait!
He could tell us he doesn't know a thing or send us a totally wrong way! There's little chance that he'll tell us the truth!
Yes, obviously! But what do we do now?
I have an idea! Listen up!

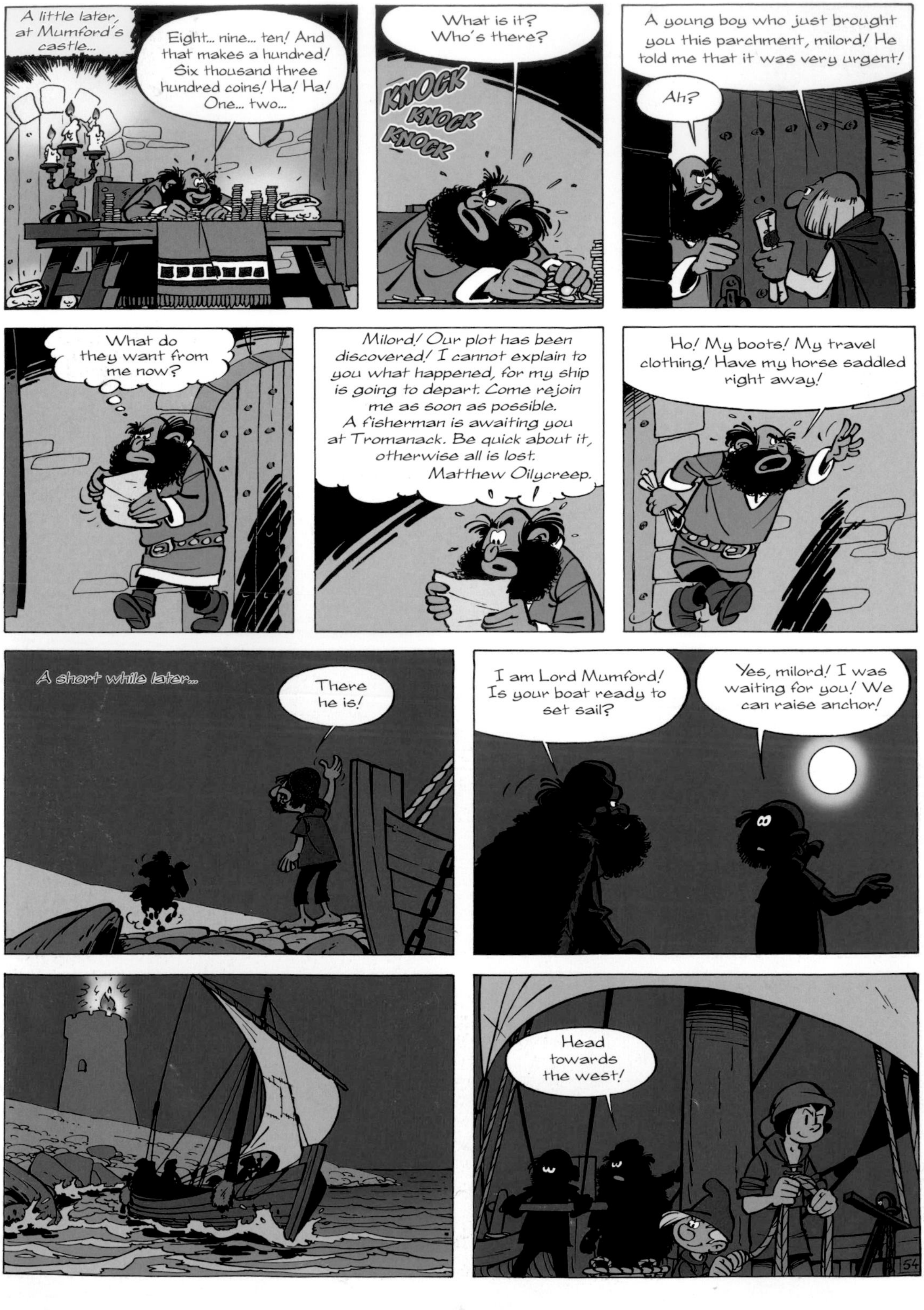
A little later, at Mumford's castle...
Eight... nine... ten! And that makes a hundred! Six thousand three hundred coins! Ha! Ha! One... two...
What is it? Who's there?
KNOCK KNOCK KNOCK
A young boy who just brought you this parchment, milord! He told me that it was very urgent!
Ah?
What do they want from me now?
Milord! Our plot has been discovered! I cannot explain to you what happened, for my ship is going to depart. Come rejoin me as soon as possible. A fisherman is awaiting you at Tromanack. Be quick about it, otherwise all is lost. Matthew Oilycreep.
Ho! My boots! My travel clothing! Have my horse saddled right away!
A short while later...
There he is!
I am Lord Mumford! Is your boat ready to set sail?
Yes, milord! I was waiting for you! We can raise anchor!
Head towards the west!
54

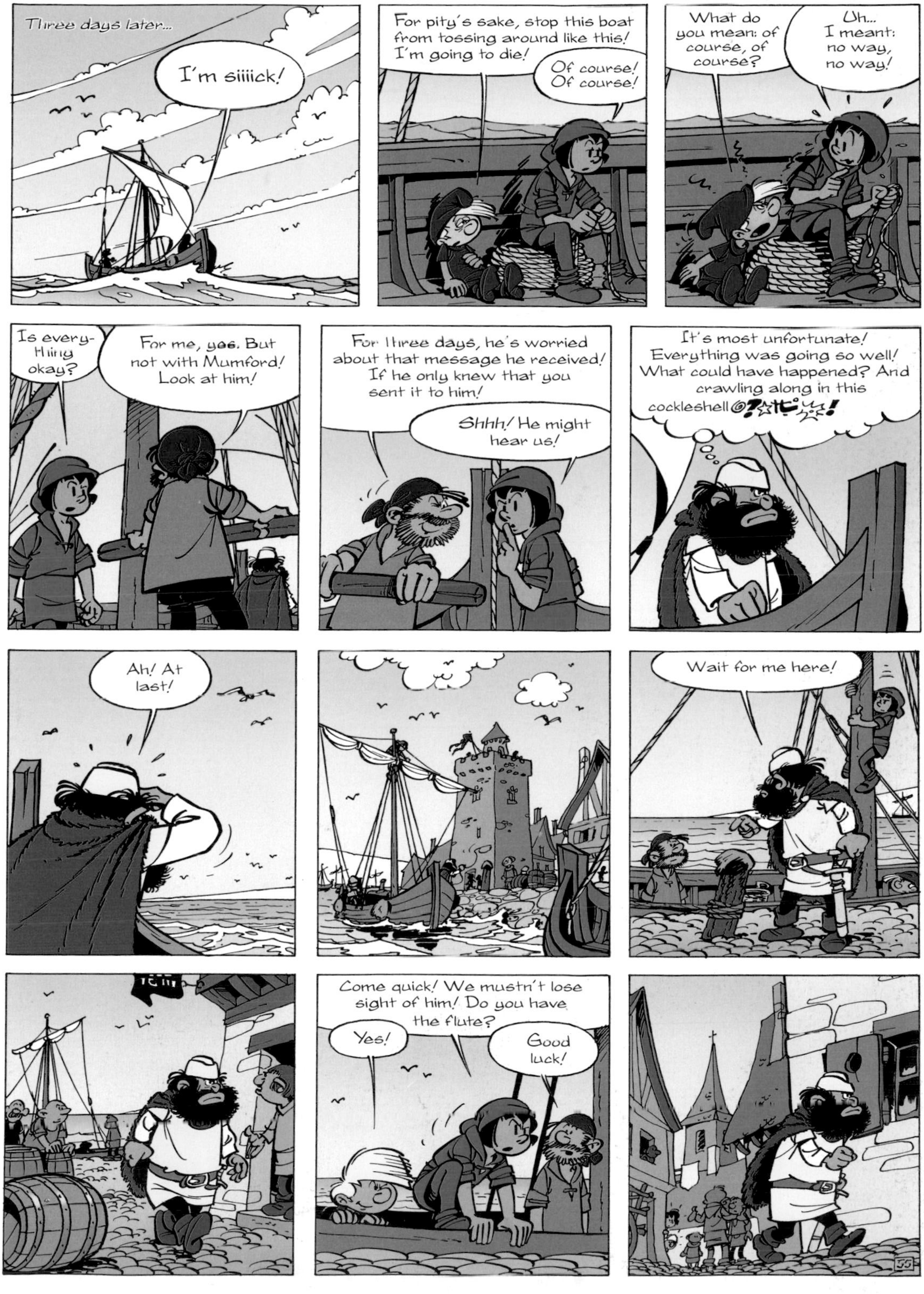
Three days later...
I'm siiiick!
For pity's sake, stop this boat from tossing around like this! I'm going to die!
Of course! Of course!
What do you mean: of course, of course?
Uh... I meant: no way, no way!
Is every-thing okay?
For me, yes. But not with Mumford! Look at him!
For three days, he's worried about that message he received! If he only knew that you sent it to him!
Shhh! He might hear us!
It's most unfortunate! Everything was going so well! What could have happened? And crawling along in this cockleshell
Ah! At last!
Wait for me here!
Come quick! We mustn't lose sight of him! Do you have the flute?
Yes!
Good luck!

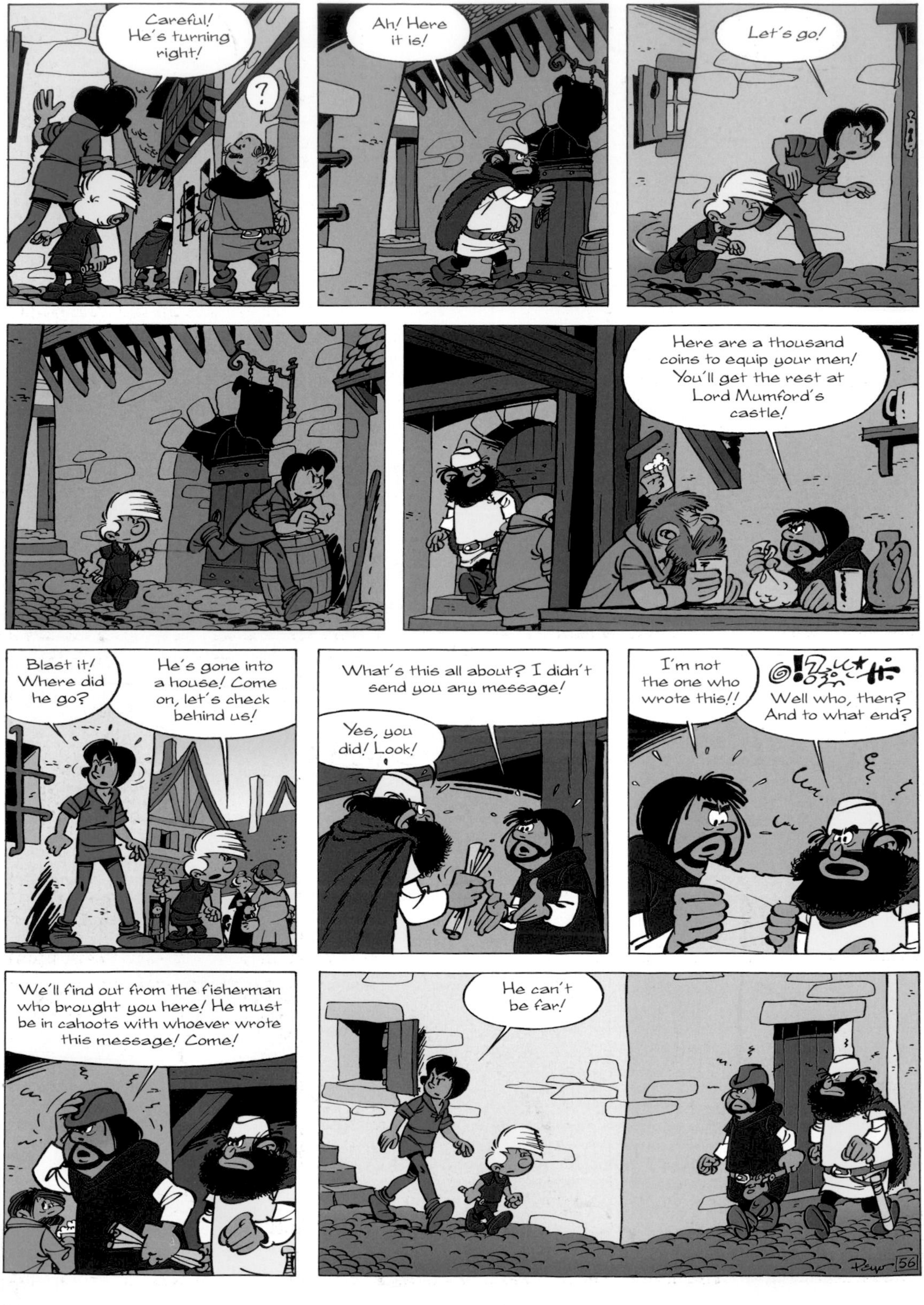
Careful! He's turning right!
?
Ah! Here it is!
Let's go!
Here are a thousand coins to equip your men! You'll get the rest at Lord Mumford's castle!
Blast it! Where did he go?
He's gone into a house! Come on, let's check behind us!
What's this all about? I didn't send you any message!
Yes, you did! Look!
I'm not the one who wrote this!!
Well who, then? And to what end?
We'll find out from the fisherman who brought you here! He must be in cahoots with whoever wrote this message! Come!
He can't be far!

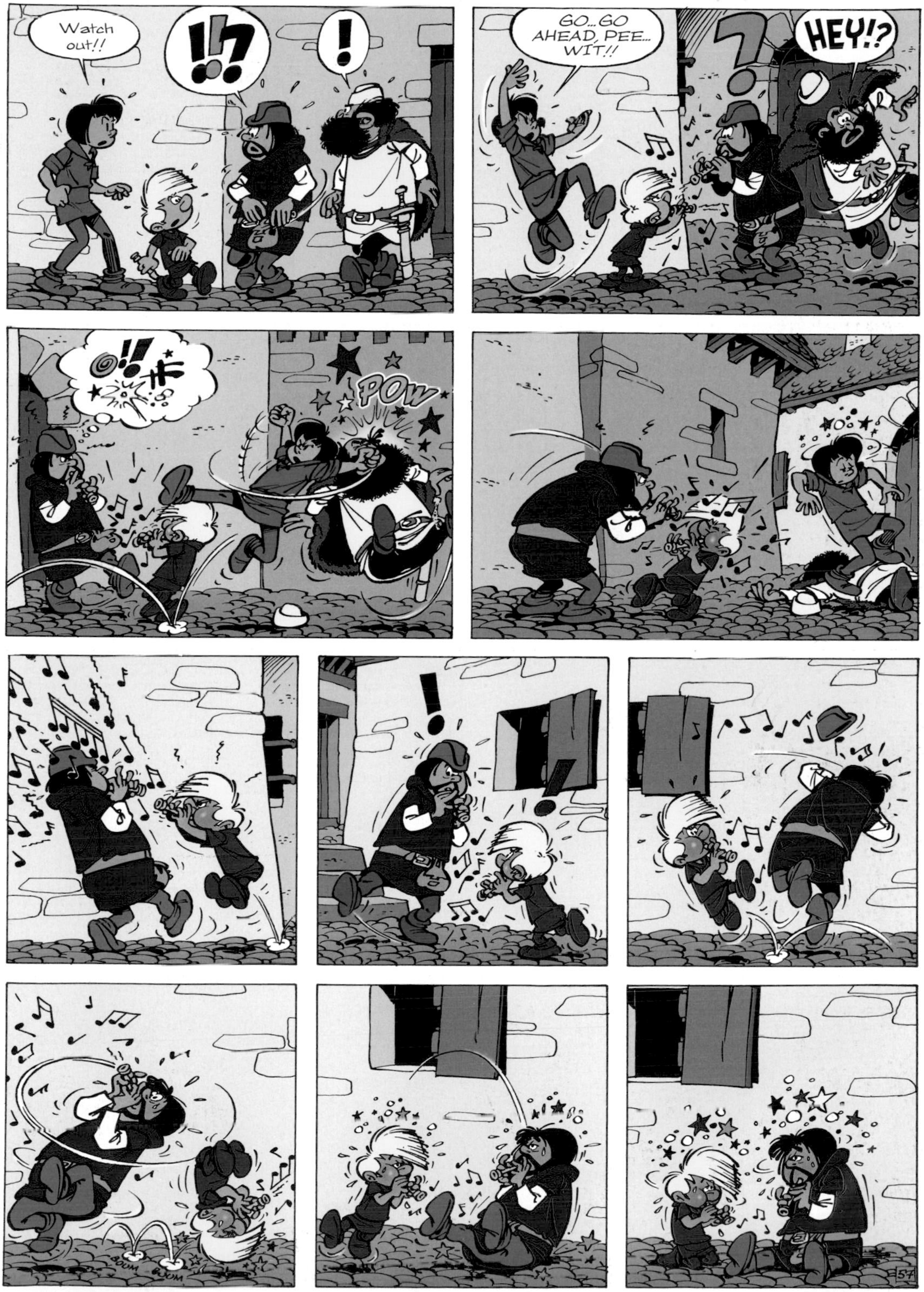
Watch out!!
!!?
!
GO... GO AHEAD, PEE... WIT!!
?
HEY!?
POW
BOUM
BOUM

⋟Puff...
puff...!⋞

⋟Puff...
puff...!⋞

⋟Whew!⋞ It's...
it's all over!
I got him!

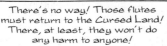

Later...

Blistering Barnacles! There's
a fortune here! Luckily we managed
to get it back before those two bandits
used it for their sinister plan!

And now we have two flutes
with holes! One for you and
one for me! We're going
have a lot of fun!

No, Peewit! We
must return those flutes
to the Smurfs!

Are you crazy?! Why?

Because they're
too dangerous! You
saw where they
led us!

All because of one little flute,
cities were ransacked, and
the country was nearly
invaded!

Mmmh!
I still feel
like keeping
one!

There's no way! Those flutes
must return to the Cursed Land!
There, at least, they won't do
any harm to anyone!

Pssst! You wouldn't have
a piece of wood, about this long,
and a knife?

Oh! Sure.
Wait! I'll find
you one.

Peyo 58

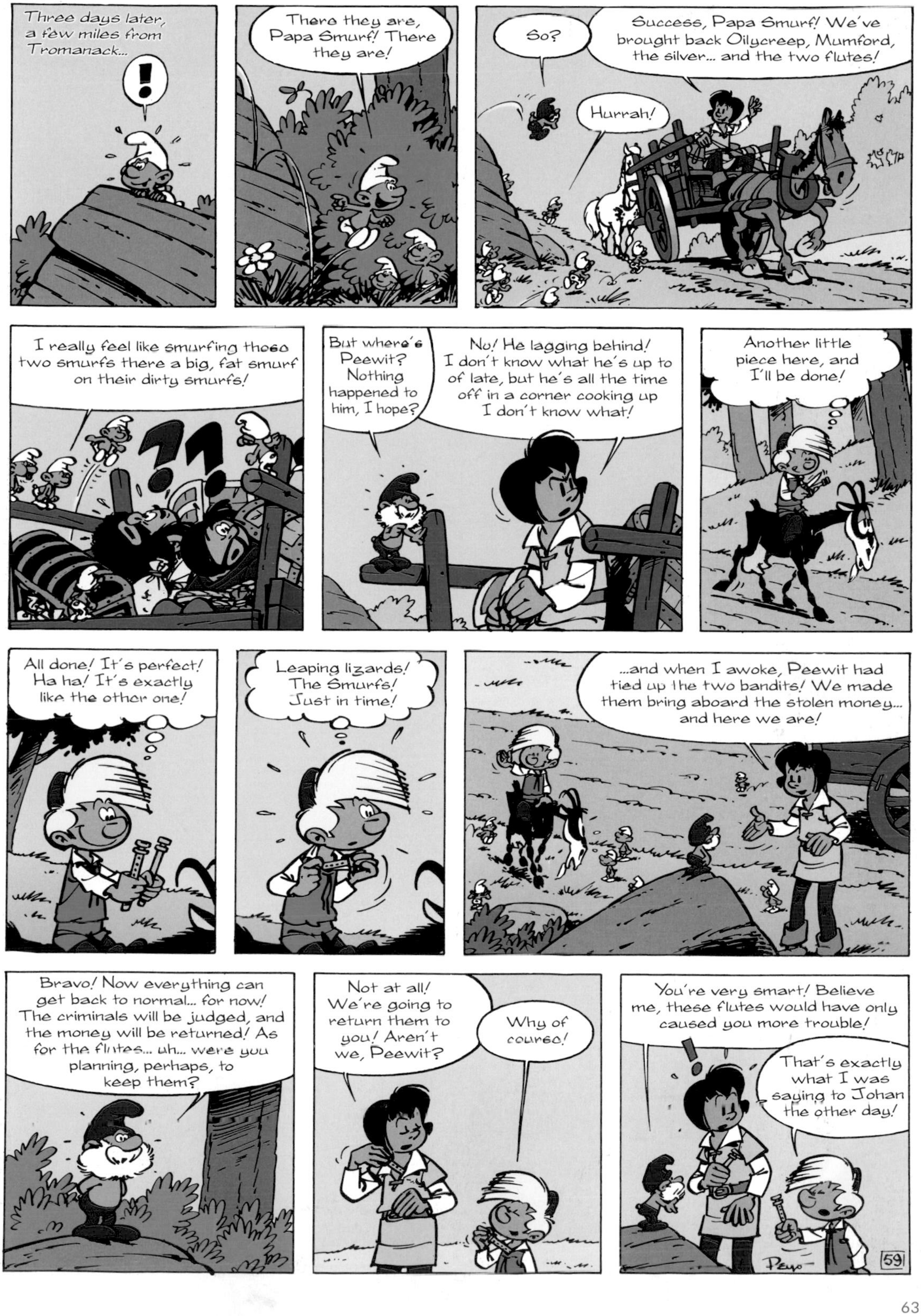

Three days later, a few miles from Tromanack...
!
There they are, Papa Smurf! There they are!
So?
Success, Papa Smurf! We've brought back Oilycreep, Mumford, the silver... and the two flutes!
Hurrah!
I really feel like smurfing those two smurfs there a big, fat smurf on their dirty smurfs!
But where's Peewit? Nothing happened to him, I hope?
No! He lagging behind! I don't know what he's up to of late, but he's all the time off in a corner cooking up I don't know what!
Another little piece here, and I'll be done!
All done! It's perfect! Ha ha! It's exactly like the other one!
Leaping lizards! The Smurfs! Just in time!
...and when I awoke, Peewit had tied up the two bandits! We made them bring aboard the stolen money... and here we are!
Bravo! Now everything can get back to normal... for now! The criminals will be judged, and the money will be returned! As for the flutes... uh... were you planning, perhaps, to keep them?
Not at all! We're going to return them to you! Aren't we, Peewit?
Why of course!
You're very smart! Believe me, these flutes would have only caused you more trouble!
!
That's exactly what I was saying to Johan the other day!
Peyo
59

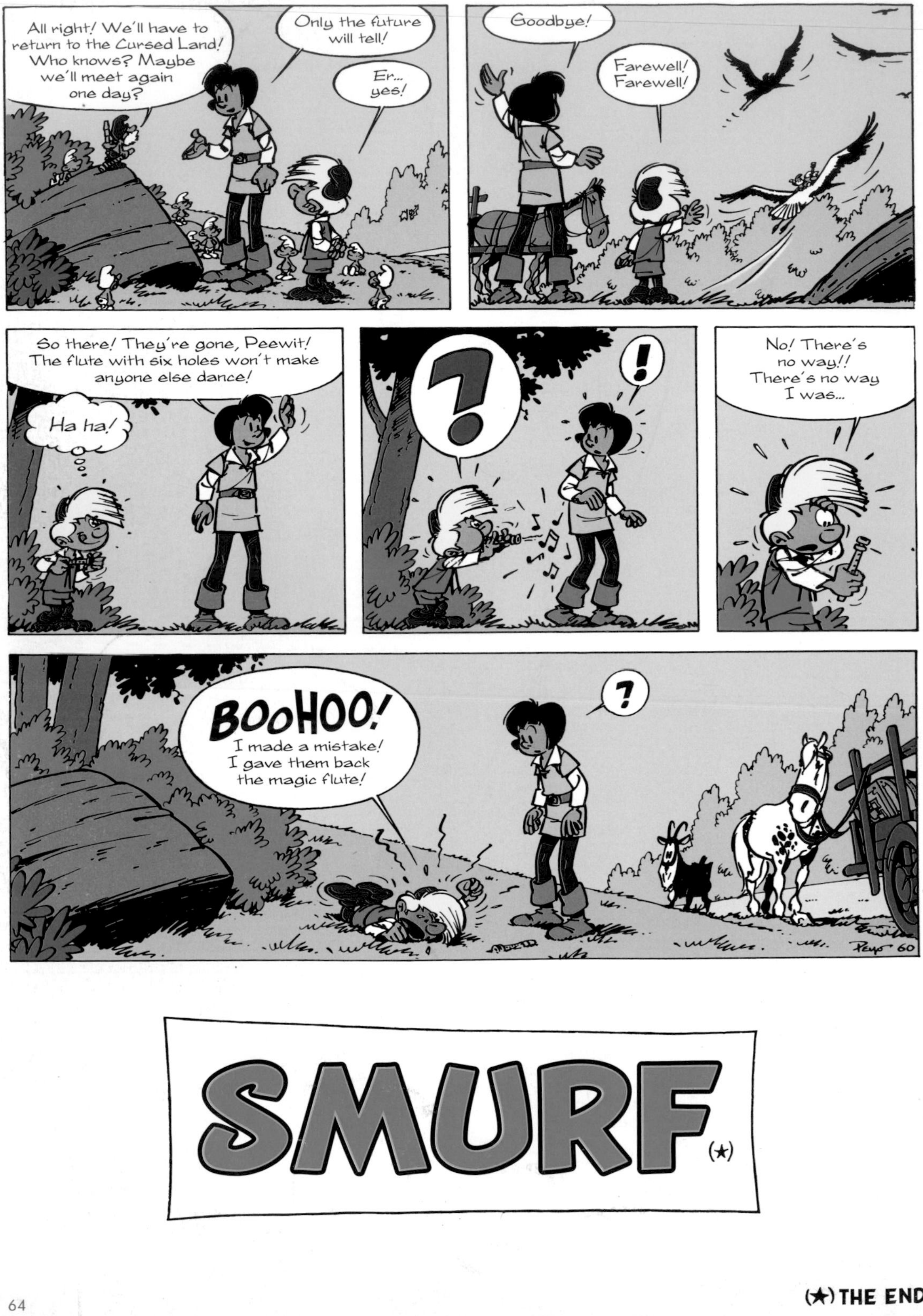
All right! We'll have to return to the Cursed Land! Who knows? Maybe we'll meet again one day?
Only the future will tell!
Er... yes!
Goodbye!
Farewell! Farewell!
So there! They're gone, Peewit! The flute with six holes won't make anyone else dance!
Ha ha!
?
!
No! There's no way!! There's no way I was...
BOOHOO! I made a mistake! I gave them back the magic flute!
?
Peyo 60

SMURF(★)

(★) THE END.

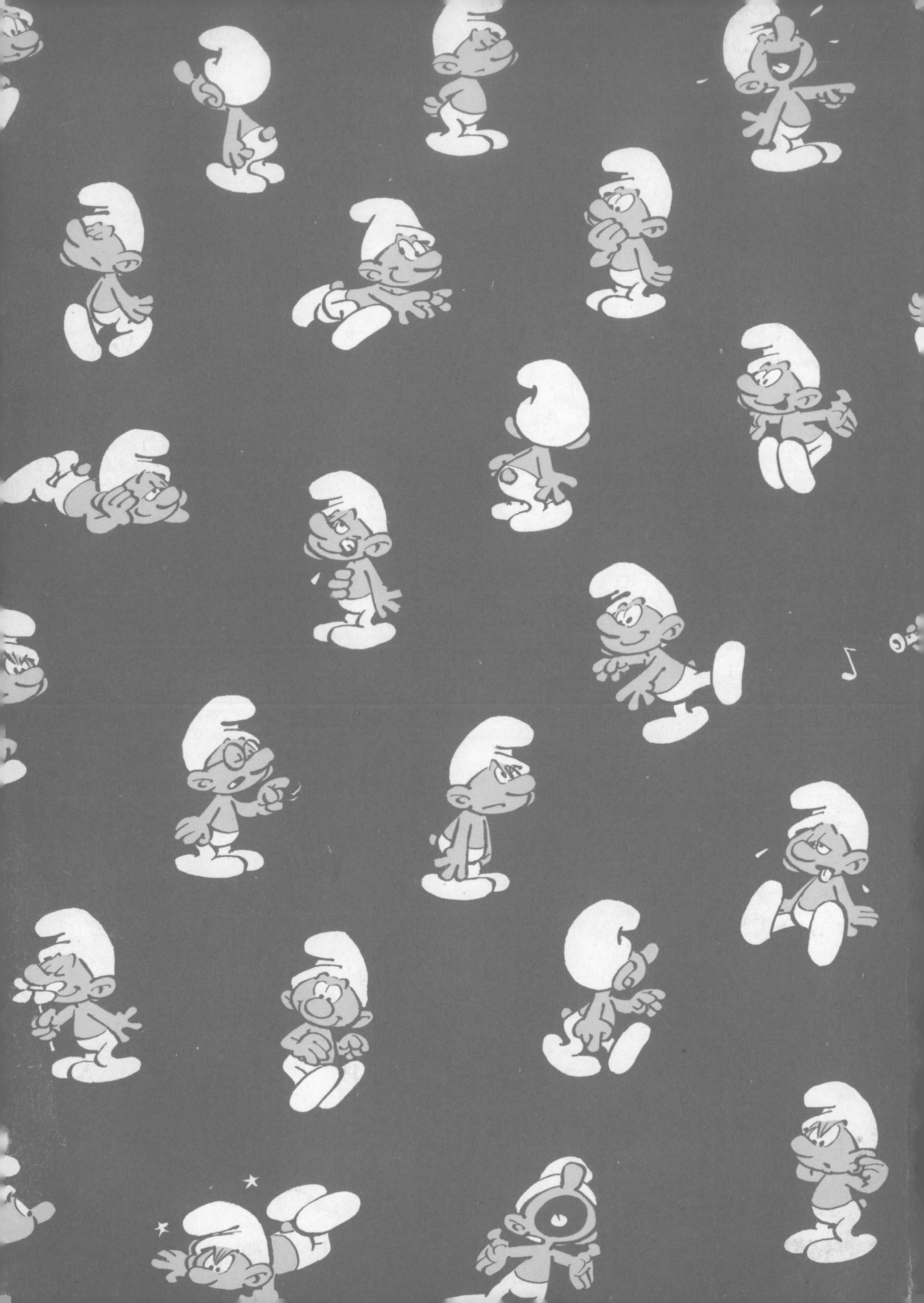